SKY CAPTAIN
AND THE WORLD
OF TOMORROW

SKY CAPTAIN AND THE WORLD OF TOMORROW

A Novel by

K. J. Anderson

Based on the Motion Picture
Written by Kerry Conran

AN ONYX BOOK

ONYX
Published by New American Library, a division of
Penguin Group (USA) Inc., 375 Hudson Street,
New York, New York 10014, U.S.A.
Penguin Books Ltd, 80 Strand,
London WC2R 0RL, England
Penguin Books Australia Ltd, 250 Camberwell Road,
Camberwell, Victoria 3124, Australia
Penguin Books Canada Ltd, 10 Alcorn Avenue,
Toronto, Ontario, Canada M4V 3B2
Penguin Books (NZ), cnr Airborne and Rosedale Roads,
Albany, Auckland 1310, New Zealand

Penguin Books Ltd, Registered Offices:
80 Strand, London WC2R 0RL, England

First published by Onyx, an imprint of New American Library,
a division of Penguin Group (USA) Inc.

First Printing, June 2004
10 9 8 7 6 5 4 3 2 1

episode 1

"MECHANICAL MONSTERS"

1

A Frightened Passenger
A Winged Skull
A Sinister Observer

In the gathering dusk, a snowstorm settled around the huge streamlined shape that eased through the cold fog.

As he stared out at the New York City skyline through the zeppelin's glass observation windows, Dr. Jorge Vargas felt as if he were trapped within an enormous snow globe, the toy of a monstrous giant.

The trapped feeling was not his imagination. And he was certainly familiar with monsters. . . .

A cold breeze rattled the panes, and he withdrew from the window, leaving a mist of condensation from his heavy, panicked breathing. From up high, the skyscrapers of Manhattan looked like a diorama in a museum display sparkling with driving white flakes.

Around him in the opulent observation lounge, other passengers sipped wine or champagne, ate expensive cheeses, chatted. One potbellied man laughed too loudly, while his companions puffed earnestly on cigars, filling the lounge with a tobacco fog nearly as thick as the blizzard outside. A band played mellow music: a clarinet, a violin, a saxophone.

The businessmen had neatly pomaded hair and immaculate tuxedos. Women showed off their pearls and jewelry; colorful cocktail dresses clung to their hips and legs, flowing like liquid fabric down to high-heeled shoes, while leaving alabaster arms and shoulders bare.

Everyone in the lounge flaunted their wealth and social status. An event of such grandeur would earn its place in history. In soirees and cocktail parties for years to come, the passengers would brag about being aboard the *Hindenburg III* on its maiden voyage from Berlin to New York City.

Dr. Vargas didn't want to be seen, however. He was simply trying to escape Germany—before it was too late.

Throughout the deceptively gentle flight over Europe and then across the wintry Atlantic, the zeppelin's chefs had astounded the wealthy passengers with exotic meals, pâtés and caviar, incredible desserts and sugary confections. Vargas, though, had little appetite. He had spent most of the time in his interior cabin, hiding, dreading. The lullaby hum of great propellers reminded him of more sinister machinery. . . .

A crewman stepped through the observation lounge on his way to the bridge. He wore a white uniform, a smart-looking cap, gold epaulets, and a mannequin smile on his clean-shaven face. He nodded to some passengers.

"Excuse me, Captain," a rail-thin woman interrupted him. She had short graying hair done up in a tight style more than a decade out-of-date, as if she had never passed beyond her days as a young flapper.

The crewman's smile barely changed. "I'm just the copilot, madam."

"Will the snowstorm delay us? Is there anything to worry about? Those buildings look very high—"

The flurry of white flakes and the gusting breezes did not seem to bother the huge dirigible. Thanks to the constant knot in his stomach, Vargas could feel any increase in the swaying motion. After the horrific explosion of the first *Hindenburg* in Lakehurst, New Jersey, two years before, everyone had good reason to be skittish.

Vargas had seen photographs of that other airship's fiery destruction after atmospheric electricity ignited a gas leak in the dirigible. (Some said the explosion was caused by anti-Nazi saboteurs.) He had seen images of the charred skeleton of the great zeppelin lying on the burned ground like the bones of a prehistoric monster. *Oh, the humanity!*

But that disaster was nothing compared to what terrors lay in store for the human race . . . if Vargas could not get away.

The copilot gave the old flapper a reassuring smile. "Not at all, madam. The *Hindenburg III* has none of the potential hazards of its predecessors. For us, even a blizzard is nothing more than frosting on the cake."

At the snow-speckled window, the woman's husband said, "Looks like frosting on the whole city down there."

The copilot was obviously well-versed in public relations. "And I think you'll agree that the amenities, the speed, and the comfort of a transatlantic voyage via zeppelin are far superior to even the finest luxury ocean liners. You mark my words, giant liners like the *Titanic* will soon be a thing of the past." Tipping his cap, the crewman walked past the couple to the polished wooden doorway that led to the bridge. "We'll be docking—safely—with the Empire State Building in under an hour."

The band continued playing. Bartenders served another round of drinks. Vargas stared out the window, clutching his dark satchel with a death grip. He carried the satchel with him everywhere he went, not daring to leave it in his cabin, even with the door locked.

Dr. Vargas was a thin, nervous man with salt-and-pepper hair, an aquiline nose, and a graying goatee. His unremarkable brown tweed suit was beginning to show too much wear. He hadn't had much chance to pack spare clothes when he'd fled Berlin.

But it wouldn't be long now. Ahead of them, spotlights crisscrossed the skyline as the zeppelin lumbered forward. The *Hindenburg III* would tie up to the world's tallest skyscraper. A brass band would welcome the passengers on the rooftop, with another one on the streets below.

Vargas would disembark with the crowd and then intentionally lose himself in the flurry of photographers and reporters. He would disappear into a city where no one knew him, where the pursuers would not guess to look for him.

Safe. For a short time at least.

The *Hindenburg III* seemed to take forever in its final approach. Passengers, many of them tipsy from too much celebrating, lined the windows of the observation lounge to gaze out at the spectacular metropolis.

When they jostled the doctor's shoulders, making him feel threatened and claustrophobic, he moved toward the back of the compartment, still clutching his satchel. At the rearmost window, the view was blocked by guy cables and the sweep of the dirigible's nearest fin. The seal of vulcanized rubber did not fit perfectly around the pane of glass, allowing a chill draft. Vargas huddled in his tweed suit, glad for the brief solitude, anxious to be off the zeppelin.

Fidgeting, he swiped a handkerchief across his brow as he discreetly eyed the room. When he was sure none of the passengers were paying any attention to him, Vargas reached into his pocket and withdrew two small test tubes.

Swallowing hard, thinking of all the work and all the dark memories that had thrown him into this dangerous situation, he let his gaze linger on the twin vials before he wrapped them in the soft folds of his handkerchief. He snapped open his satchel and placed them protectively inside.

The loudspeaker system crackled, and the captain's voice boomed out in deep, rolling German. Vargas flinched in instinctive terror, remembering other harsh commands delivered over blaring intercoms.

But the man was simply announcing the *Hindenburg III*'s imminent arrival. "All passengers please take your seats and prepare for the docking procedure. We may encounter some slight turbulence due to the snowstorm as we dock to the Empire State Building."

Outside, louder than the thrumming of the zeppelin's impressive motors, came the drone of airplane engines. Six swift fighter aircraft, each one painted with intimidating insignia—tiger stripes, leopard spots, or a red mouth of snarling fangs—roared past the gliding *Hindenburg*.

Vargas quailed, but the other passengers whistled and cheered. The six aircraft sped past, tilting their wings in friendly acknowledgment. The captain came back over the loudspeaker. "Ladies and gentlemen, we are fortunate to receive a ceremonial escort from the famous Flying Legion! If any of you had doubts that we would arrive safely, I trust they are now put to rest?"

Vargas knew the heroics of the mercenary Flying Legion. The daredevil fliers had saved the world from numerous threats, whether it was deadly comet dust or mad scientists with super weapons or bank robbers with machines that tunneled through the Earth's crust. He let out a brief sigh of relief.

Two eager boys ran playfully past the old man, bounding to the only uncrowded window. Adults formed an impenetrable barricade at each of the prime observation spots.

"Let me see! Let me see!"

"Is Sky Captain with them?"

As Vargas drew back, the boys bumped him and knocked his satchel to the deck. Since he hadn't clicked the clasp shut, the case broke open, spilling papers. The doctor snapped at the boys, "Please, please! You must be careful!"

But the youngsters were too eager to watch the daring maneuvers of the Flying Legion planes to pay much attention to the old man. As Vargas frantically scooped up his scattered papers, he doubted any casual observer would see significance in all the documents. But to him the schematics and diagrams of complex mechanical components held dire significance for the future of the world.

Each paper bore a prominent, ominous emblem stamped in the upper right corner—a grinning skull framed by iron-feathered wings. He grabbed the documents, covering the winged skull before anyone could see it.

At the bottom of the pile lay a grisly autopsy photo. Vargas froze, remembering the victim's pitiful cries, the awful experiment. He feared he might vomit right there in the observation lounge (which the other passengers would no doubt attribute to airsickness). Then he glanced up to see one of the boys staring at the photograph, horrified. Before the boy could call out to his companion, Vargas stuffed the autopsy photograph in the satchel and fled. He couldn't get off the zeppelin soon enough.

As the passengers gathered their belongings, talked to stewards, and waited for the final docking, Vargas moved down the *Hindenburg*'s passageways, looking right and left. Close to his chest so no one could see, he held a pencil and a scrap of paper, on which he hastily scribbled a note. He glanced at the bustling porters assisting with baggage; he was searching for one in particular. He finally spotted the familiar man with blond hair, a rough complexion, and an easy smile.

When Vargas caught the porter's eye, the other man nodded. "Yes, Dr. Vargas?"

The doctor kept his voice low, pressing the satchel into the porter's callused hands. "This parcel must be delivered the moment we reach port. I . . . won't be able to do it myself." Passengers milled around them, and Vargas swallowed hard. He clasped his own hands around the porter's, forcing him to grip the case's handle. "A man will be waiting at this address—Dr. Walter Jennings. You must see that the satchel is placed in his hands. Personally. There can be no mistake."

"Yes, Doctor. Right away." The porter lifted his jaw to show his determination.

During the long journey, the porter had been cordial, not overinquisitive or solicitous, but he had sensed this passenger's deep anxiety. Perhaps it was desperation, perhaps it was foolhardiness, but Dr. Vargas had decided to trust the man. Vargas had no allies, no other choice—and the risk was too great to count on achieving everything alone. He needed assistance, and that porter had no connection whatsoever with Unit Eleven or their diabolical creations. He had taken the chance.

The poor porter knew only the vaguest details of what he'd gotten into. Vargas felt sorry for endangering the man, but he had no choice. It was a long time since he'd been accustomed to dealing with *innocent* people.

Taking the satchel casually, as if it were just another piece of luggage, the porter walked away, leaving Vargas standing by the window, feigning nonchalance. Finally, when he was far enough away, the porter glanced at the slip of paper Dr. Vargas had curled around the handle of the small bag.

HE KNOWS I'M HERE.
YOU MUST PROTECT THEM.
GOOD-BYE, MY FRIEND.

The porter blinked with concern. He hadn't believed how serious the scientist's spy games were. He turned back to where the old man had been staring forlornly out the window.

Dr. Vargas had vanished into the crowd of passengers.

Spotlights blazed against the zeppelin as it cruised above Manhattan and approached its destination. Continually falling snow reflected the bright beams of light, sparkling around the *Hindenburg*'s smooth exterior. From the skyscraper's rooftop, newspaper reporters took flash photographs. In the streets below, crowds looked up to point at the massive dirigible coming to dock at the world's tallest structure.

A team of men standing at the zenith of the Empire State Building gathered the towing lines suspended below the zeppelin's belly. Straining with the snow-wet ropes, they ushered the lighter-than-air ship to the sheltered dock.

When the vessel had settled into position one hundred stories above New York City, a gangplank was lowered into place, then anchored for stability. Passengers, pleased to be among the first to disembark on the craft's maiden voyage, moved down the suspended bridge. Though the wide walkway was guarded with grip ropes, the plank spanned a dizzying height between the *Hindenburg III* and the building. Most of the passengers could not stop themselves from looking down. . . .

Far below, at the base of the skyscraper, a dark figure watched the activity above. Standing on the corner of Thirty-fourth Street and Fifth Avenue, the stranger stared upward with all the other people, but this person remained silent and isolated. Though other pedestrians shivered in the cold from the falling snow, the shrouded figure was impervious to the weather.

Eventually, a black-gloved hand produced a small notebook from within a heavy jacket. Seven names were written in the notebook in precise block letters, every line even. There were no other notes, no markings. Five of the names had lines drawn through them.

The dark figure raised a quill and methodically crossed out the sixth name on the list: DOKTOR JORGE VARGAS. Then the notebook was snapped shut and tucked away into the jacket.

Only one name remained.

2

An Intrepid Reporter
A String of Disappearances
A Mysterious Package

Hot off the presses!

At her desk in the *Chronicle* offices, Polly Perkins lifted her fresh copy of the early edition, scanning the front page. She loved the feel of crisp newspaper, the oily smell of black ink, the sound of rustling pages as she shuffled through the sections. Each copy carried the heady excitement of *news*. Sometimes she even went to the cavernous printing factories and stood in front of the rumbling newspaper presses just so she could snatch one of the first copies to come down the line.

Especially if the edition contained an article or a photograph she had contributed. Like today's.

New York's tall buildings filled the window behind her, but she leaned closer to the yellow glow of her desk lamp. The lamp's body was an illuminated frosted-glass globe of Earth. She had never been able to decide if it was an innovative art deco design or pure kitsch. Either way, the lamp served its purpose.

Polly unfolded the front page of the newspaper, engrossed. The headline in bold seventy-point type, heavy block letters, shouted triumphantly:

HINDENBURG III DOCKED WITH EMPIRE
MAIDEN VOYAGE OF AIRSHIP

A photograph—made grainy either by the snow flurries or poor reproduction—showed the prominent zeppelin tethered to the top of the skyscraper, like a plaything for Willis O'Brien's *King Kong*. Another photo, taken by a hardy amateur journalist who had stood out in the blizzard, showed the *Hindenburg III* from a distance framed by the towers and suspension cables of the Brooklyn Bridge.

Polly ignored the huge headline, though, and considered a small article on the bottom of the page, which was much more important to her. She turned the newspaper over, leaning close and smiling as she scanned the words, alert for typographical errors.

POLICE SEEK MISSING SCIENTIST
by Polly Perkins

Her blue eyes lingered on the byline before turning to the rest of the article. Accompanying the text was another grainy photograph, at least ten years old, but it was the best she could find in all the *Chronicle*'s archives. Dr. Jorge Vargas had apparently disappeared as soon as the zeppelin docked, and she hoped readers might be able to identify the man, even if the picture was out-of-date.

It would be quite a scoop if she could find him herself.

Demure and unflappable, Polly was the *Chronicle*'s crack investigative reporter—at least she considered herself to be. Her editor, Morris Paley, suggested she still needed a few more credentials. As soon as he'd said that, his baggy eyes suddenly lit up in alarm. "Now, Polly, that doesn't mean I want you to get yourself in trouble!"

"I don't want to get in trouble, Mr. Paley. I want to get the *news*. Sometimes you have to do one to accomplish the other." She had smiled and shooed him away so she could get back to her typing on a well-used black Royal typewriter. Editor Paley had lingered at the office doorway, paternally worried about her, but Polly had ignored him. With her icy coolness, she would one day convince him that she could take care of herself. . . .

Now, turning back to her typewriter, she became lost in her own thought, her fingers pounding the keys furiously. Dr. Vargas was just the latest in a disturbing string of disappearances of prominent scientists who had worked in Germany for decades. She had noticed the connection and tracked down five other incidents where researchers had inexplicably vanished. Polly had written several articles, and Editor Paley had printed them, sometimes prominently and other times at the back of the section.

So far, she hadn't managed to create much of a hue and cry. Nobody else believed the seriousness of the situation, but someone out there must have been reading and wondering. This latest disappearance seemed even more suspicious than the other five. With all the details she'd pieced together, it was plain to her that Dr. Vargas had been attempting to flee something. . . .

The intercom on Polly's desk buzzed, and she stopped typing to flip the switch.

"There's a package for you, Miss Perkins."

"Thanks, Isabel. I'll be right there."

Down in the *Chronicle* lobby, Polly rapped her fingers impatiently on the front desk. Her wavy golden hair was neat and perfect, partially pinned up with barrettes, but she did not waste her time with complicated and fashionable new styles. She wore a smart business dress and black shoes with sensible low heels that would allow her to run after a story (or run *from* one, if the circumstances turned out badly). Polly had a catlike mouth with full red lips, a delicately pointed nose, and a calm, strong beauty that set her apart from the wilting, giggling lovelies who spent their days trying to snag the attentions of men.

The lobby receptionist, on the other hand, walked like a wiggling duck in her tight red dress and high heels as she returned from the storeroom with a small brown package. "Here you are, Miss Perkins."

Polly took the package with a curious frown. "I'm not expecting anything, Isabel. Do you know who—"

"They didn't leave a name. Said it was important." As Polly hefted the package, then tore the paper away to reveal an old hardcover book, Isabel leaned over her counter. "Is that one of those new bestseller novels?"

Polly glanced at the title stamped in gold foil on a leatherette cover. *Mathematical Principles of Natural Philosophy* by Sir Isaac Newton.

"I don't think so, Isabel. Something a bit more classic."

In truth, she had no idea what it could mean. Curious, she flipped open the front cover to find a loose movie theater ticket for an evening showing of *The Wizard of Oz*. A note had been hastily scribbled on the inside jacket in thin, spidery letters:

I know who's next. Meet me tonight at 6:00. Come alone!

3

The Editor and the Gun
A Clandestine Meeting
A Missed Opportunity

Reporters were good at protecting sources and keeping secrets. Working for the *Chronicle* was a tough business, and Polly had learned how to avoid obstacles or knock them aside. Not long after she received her mysterious message, she crept into her dimly lighted office and moved toward a row of filing cabinets. In the dim illumination, the beehive of Manhattan's lights began to glow through the window behind her. Although the newspaper offices were quiet after the close of business, Polly moved with unnecessary furtiveness. She slid open the top drawer of the filing cabinet and reached inside as far as her arm would go to rummage behind the file folders. From the back she withdrew a gilded oak box and brought it to her desk, where she moved pencils and notepads aside. With the fingernail of her index finger, she popped open the catch and lifted the lid of the case.

"I've got a job for you tonight—I hope," she said to the small camera that rested neatly inside the padding. Polly gingerly lifted the camera out of the box, expertly checked the mechanism, loaded fresh film, clicked the shutter, and adjusted the lens cap. Satisfied, she slung the leather camera strap over her shoulder. The camera was a vital tool of the trade, her secret weapon to be used only for the most important stories. And if this strange message in Newton's book had anything to do with the missing scientists, she didn't want to take any chances. . . .

With the Leica ready to go, Polly dug even deeper in the back of the filing cabinet and pulled out a .45 caliber Colt service revolver and a small box of bullets. She suspected there might be some shooting tonight— either with the camera or the revolver.

She swung open the revolver's cylinder and casually spun it. She had loaded two of the six empty chambers when someone suddenly flipped on the lights. Momentarily blinded but moving with swift reflexes, Polly spun around, holding the revolver ready.

Standing in the doorway was a gray-haired man in his late sixties. Completely undisturbed by the gun pointed at him, Editor Paley let out a long, slow sigh and shook his head. "Polly, why do you do this to me? Where did I go wrong as your editor?"

Nonchalantly, Polly continued to feed bullets into the revolver. "This?" She raised the heavy gun. "Colt New Service M1917. It's just a toy. My grandma gave it to me."

"I'm sending one of the boys with you. I don't like this business you're getting yourself into." He gestured to the revolver. "And *that* stays here. No arguments."

Polly didn't have any intention of arguing . . . or listening. "I'll be fine, Mr. Paley. You know what a careful girl I am." She spun the cylinder shut and stuffed the Colt into her shoulder bag.

"My mouth moves, words come out, and you don't hear them."

"Oh, I hear them." She caught a glimpse of the big clock on the wall, then grabbed her bag and headed for the door. "I'm late for a movie. *The Wizard of Oz*—have you seen it?"

"I hear it's good, but I doubt it can compete with

Gone with the Wind. My wife liked that one." Editor Paley had three grown daughters, none of whom had ever given him any trouble; Polly, though, wasn't anything like them. When she flashed a smile that made him flinch, he said, "Polly, I don't like it when you smile at me."

"You don't like my smile?" She smiled again, brighter this time.

"I don't like what's behind it." He stopped her at the door, but he knew he couldn't block her way when she was determined. As a last resort, he tried to be reasonable. "Six scientists are missing, Polly—probably dead. Someone out there means business, and I don't want you in the middle of it. It's time you leave the detective work to the police."

"I'm only going to a movie, Mr. Paley. Munchkins, cowardly lions, tin woodsmen—"

"Uh-huh. With a gun and a camera."

"A girl can't be too careful these days. You don't have to worry about me."

"I'm worried for *me*. If you get yourself killed, there's a lot of paperwork involved. And then I have to start from scratch training your replacement." He rubbed his heavy cheeks, pensive. "Of course, maybe somebody else would be a bit less intractable. . . ."

Polly flippantly moved past him. "I'll bring you back some popcorn."

As she went by, the editor insisted on giving her a reassuring hug, barely more than a pat, and Polly indulged him. His hand brushed her leather bag.

After she had gone, Morris Paley's expression showed no defeat. "You've still got a lot of tricks to learn about this business, kid." In his right hand, he smugly twirled the Colt, which he had easily lifted from her bag. "I hope you live long enough to master them all."

*　　*　　*

Pinkish-orange neon lights spelled out the letters of Radio City Music Hall. The usual throng of city dwellers passed by the theater going about their daily business. The streets were wet and sloppy with melting snow. Yellow cabs raced by, splashing slush as they stopped at the curb to let out theatergoers.

Polly climbed out the back of a cab, bent into the window to pay the driver, then turned to face Radio City. She wore a black fedora over her long blond hair and a warm trench coat to hide her camera strap. She glanced at her watch again. She didn't want to be late. Polly walked purposefully toward the door, bypassing the ticket window. She didn't even notice as her cab raced away, splattering other pedestrians.

In front of the theater, an elaborate display advertised the new film everyone was talking about, *The Wizard of Oz*. Polly had heard rave reviews, but hadn't found time to see the movie. Talking scarecrows and heartless tin men weren't really her style. But she was supposed to meet her contact here.

An usher took the ticket Polly had found inside the Isaac Newton volume. As she entered the lobby of the theater, several men gave her appreciative looks, but none showed any special sign of recognition. The man who had left the brief, intriguing message inside the book must be there waiting. Suspicious of everyone, clearly trying to make contact with anybody who would meet her eyes, she moved slowly through the foyer.

She settled into a place near the concession stand where she could scan the crowd, then reached into her handbag and withdrew the book. Maybe the man had only read Polly Perkins's byline and didn't know what she looked like. She held the book out in front of her, careful to keep it prominently displayed by tilting it this way and that.

Most of the patrons didn't even notice her, and

those who did responded only with curious looks. A well-dressed man bumped Polly on his way to purchase popcorn. She held out the book for him to see, but when he read the title, he gave her a sour look and stepped to the concession stand. When he had turned away, Polly made a face at him.

Sighing, she again glanced around the foyer—and this time noticed a man standing in the shadows of the balcony staircase. He was clutching a small satchel. She sensed something about him. . . .

Their eyes locked. The man turned and started up the stairway, apparently intending for her to follow. Trying not to be too obvious, Polly waited a moment, then trotted up the winding stairs after him.

As if afraid to look at her again, the man did not turn around, but moved directly toward a row of empty seats at the front of the balcony. It was not a very good place to view the show, but the seats did provide a place for private conversation. The movie had already started, and as she followed the man down the empty aisle, she glanced up to observe Judy Garland clutching a small dog to her chest as she walked through a decidedly exotic locale. The actress told the dog that she didn't think they were in Kansas anymore, which seemed an astute observation, given the circumstances.

She settled into the seat next to the man. He was thin and nervous, with gray hair and the face of an absentminded professor. In the flickering light from the movie screen, Polly saw that he had darting brown eyes behind gold-rimmed spectacles. They sat stiffly beside each other, silent but tense, like two teenagers on a first date.

Finally, Polly held up the book. "You sent me this?"

He glanced quickly around to make sure the nearby seats were all empty, then nodded.

Emboldened and sensing a story, Polly asked, "Who are you? What's this all about, Mister . . .?"

"Dr. . . . Dr. Walter Jennings. But keep your voice down please." The man had a clear German accent.

Polly obliged. "What kind of doctor are you? A surgeon?"

"I'm a research chemist. I specialize in nucleic acid emissions. The bonding enzymes in proteus molecules which—"

Now her suspicions were verified. "The missing scientists! You said you knew who was next."

He hesitated. "Yes . . . I . . ."

They sat a long time without saying another word. She could already tell he needed more incentive to spill everything he knew. Polly stood up and then turned to exit. "Doctor, you contacted *me*. I have a deadline to meet. If you don't intend to talk—"

Jennings clutched the sleeve of her trench coat. "All right, listen to me. I was one of seven scientists chosen to serve in a secret facility stationed outside of Berlin before the beginning of the Great War. It was known only as Einheit Elf, Unit Eleven. We agreed never to discuss what went on behind those doors." His voice was distant. "The things we were made to do there . . . terrible things."

Polly began to scribble notes on her pad. When the scientist saw what she was doing, he paused, frightened again. Behind his spectacles, tears glimmered in his eyes. "I . . . I really shouldn't have come. . . ." He rose and bolted in the opposite direction, threading his way past the empty seats to reach the aisle, where he could scuttle out the back.

After those tantalizing comments, Polly had no intention of letting the man get away. She caught up to the scientist and grabbed his arm. "Wait! In your note, you said you knew who was next. Six scientists have already vanished."

"Yes . . . I . . ." His expression fell. "Don't you see? There is only one left."

"Who is it? Who?"

"Me. He's coming for *me!*"

Suddenly, with a din that penetrated even the noise of the movie, air-raid sirens began to blare from the surrounding rooftops. The piercing wail of New York's civil defense warnings ramped up and down with a warbling tone that struck fear into all men, women, and children. The film on the wide movie screen flickered, then stopped. The house lights came up as air-raid sirens transformed the theater into a riot scene.

Terrified, Jennings struggled, but Polly would not let go of his arm. "Who, Doctor? *Who's* coming?" People in the audience began to scream louder than the sirens.

Jennings's eyes lit in terror. "Totenkopf! It's Totenkopf!"

Polly strained to remember the little bit of German she knew. Totenkopf. Dead Head? Death's Head?

The scientist yanked his arm away so forcefully that he tore the outer seam of his jacket. "I have to get out of here! He has found me!"

Panicked theatergoers streamed from the upper balcony and ran for the exits, crowding between Jennings and Polly. She could no longer reach him. The scientist glanced back at her, his gold-rimmed eyeglasses askew. Then he moved down the stairs, swept away with the crowd.

Evacuation alarms continued to wail, but Polly had other concerns than an imminent bombardment from the skies. Turning back to where she'd been sitting, she noticed something out of the corner of her eye. A folded sheet of paper had fallen from Dr. Jennings's satchel—by accident, or intentionally?—and lodged in the theater seat.

Oblivious to the chaos around her as the balcony

emptied, Polly picked up the paper. When she unfolded it, she stared at the schematic drawing of a strange machine. From the scale marks on the drawing, she was sure she must be interpreting the blueprint incorrectly. The size didn't seem possible.

Perplexed, Polly turned back to the exit through which Jennings had just fled. Outside, she heard the menacing rumble of something huge approaching.

4

Robots from the Sky
The Defense of Manhattan
Polly Gets Her Scoop

When Polly burst out of the movie theater into the street, she ran into a scene of complete mayhem. Cabs skidded into one another, scraping sparks and denting bumpers. Pedestrians ran headlong into the roadways, blindly seeking shelter.

Though America was not at war with any nation, every year it seemed another mad scientist with another doomsday plan tried to destroy a major city. Polly remembered the flying Iron Sphere and its mind-control antennae, and then it was Lord Dynamo and his terrible lightning-rod zeppelin. By now the population of Manhattan had learned how to react in an emergency. Air-raid sirens pealed out, and New Yorkers raced for designated civil defense shelters.

Called into position by spotters stationed atop the tallest skyscrapers, military and police battalions hurriedly set up defensive blockades. They prepared their weapons and set up cars and tanks as roadblocks. Piercing spotlights swept the darkening skies, searching for the oncoming threat.

A droning, thunderous rumble echoed through the canyons of the city, sounds reflected by the tall buildings. Policemen and soldiers tilted the barrels of their guns high. Terrified people simply pointed their fingers and stared upward.

Polly peered into the slice of sky visible between buildings and saw an aerial invasion force unlike any she had ever imagined. A swarm of strange flying machines cruised overhead, shaped not like aircraft, but metal *humans* with legs pressed together and arms outstretched as wings. The giant metal men cruised along under their own power, organized in a tight formation descending over New York.

Polly ducked around the corner of a building as uniformed soldiers ran past, their boots clattering on the wet sidewalk. They held rifles and machine guns ready as if they were charging enemy trenches in the Great War. Fifth Avenue was fast becoming a battle zone.

Moving with a reporter's automatic instincts, Polly had already removed her camera, installed the electronic flash, and snapped a quick photo of the mayhem. At least she had plenty of film. But she needed to see more—and she had to get her story off to the *Chronicle* before any other reporter got the scoop. By sheer dumb luck, because of her meeting with Dr. Jennings, Polly Perkins was right in the thick of things. Editor Paley would be proud . . . or angry.

Like a flock of sinister migrating geese, the giant robots droned overhead higher than the skyscrapers, heading toward an unknown target. Wave after wave of them passed.

As she considered her next move, Polly spotted a phone booth on the corner of Fifty-third Street and made a run for it. Tucking herself inside, she slid the folding glass door shut to block out most of the uproar of air-raid sirens and military preparations. She urgently produced a handful of change from her purse, deposited a coin into the phone's slot, then dialed.

Polly pressed the receiver close to her ear as Editor Paley's phone rang. She knew the older man would still be there. In fact, in such an emergency, he was probably standing at his window along with a few other reporters, watching searchlights scan the heavens and trying to make sense of the ominous fleet of flying iron giants.

On the third ring, Paley picked up the phone. "City desk!" In the background, she could hear that the newsroom was in a chaotic frenzy.

"It's Polly, Mr. Paley! I'm your reporter on the scene. Right here, in the midst of it all."

"Polly?" He didn't sound pleased at all. "Listen to me—you get out of there!"

"That doesn't sound like a good decision, Mr. Paley. Don't you want to sell newspapers?"

He grumbled. "Tell me what's going on. They're calling for Midtown to evacuate."

With rapid-fire chatter, Polly explained while flipping through pages in her small notepad. "Listen, Mr. Paley, I don't have much time. I met with my contact in the theater and got some information. Everything ties together with the disappearances. I'm sure of it."

"What ties together? What are you talking about, Polly?"

Watching the military tanks pull into position, she wedged the phone between her shoulder and ear so she could scribble another note. "I need anything you can dig up for me on a Dr. Walter Jennings and someone named Totenkopf. A project named Unit Eleven. Get me a phone number, an address, anything you can find. It's important."

"Totenkopf? Who is he?"

"That's what I'm hoping you can tell me. A German researcher or something. I think he may be involved with the missing scientists. Meanwhile, I'll see what I can find out around here."

"Uh, Polly—you do know they've set up a restricted perimeter? You're supposed to evacuate."

"I'm supposed to get a scoop for the *Chronicle*, Mr. Paley, so don't ask me to leave now."

On the phone, she heard him call to a copy boy and bark orders. "You there, dig up some information on this—fast as you can." His voice became louder as he spoke directly into the phone again. "Polly, listen to me. I'm your boss, and I want you out of there right now. Do you hear me? Hang up the phone, close your notebook, and just get out of there."

Polly turned to look through the window of the phone booth. "Wait a minute. . . . I see something." Her eyes widened. "It's coming into sight now above the Palisades! They're . . . they're huge! They're crossing Sixth Avenue. Fifth Avenue. A hundred . . . a hundred yards away."

From inside the phone booth, Polly moved her eyes slowly upward, amazed at the massive size of the machines heading her way. They were taller than some of the buildings. Her voice dropped to a whisper. "My God . . ."

Desperate gunfire erupted all around her.

At the *Chronicle*'s city desk, Morris Paley could hear the chaos through the telephone receiver. Out of his office window, he saw bright spotlights and the sparkling flicker of repeated gunfire from ground level. He clutched the phone. "Polly?" There was no answer. "Polly!"

On the corner of Fifty-third Street, the receiver swung freely inside the empty phone booth. The editor's faint voice called after her through the dangling telephone. "Polly! Polly!"

5

March of the Giant Machines
Calling Sky Captain!
A Dangerous Photo Opportunity

While the police hunkered down in formation behind their squad cars, preparing to open fire, Polly sprinted away from the phone booth. Her camera dangled on its strap, and she knew she had to get closer—but the police barricade was right in her way. Everyone else had already evacuated or found secure shelter.

Her shadow cast a trim silhouette against the brick foundation of a tenement building as she ran down a narrow alleyway, sneaking around the squad cars.

"Stop! Hey, lady—come back!" A police officer blew a whistle at her. "Aww, c'mon, lady! I can't go chasing after you—we got giant monsters coming this way!"

Polly didn't answer as she caught her breath in the darkened alley, then checked her camera, ready for the best shot. She would do whatever it took to get the story or snap an award-winning photograph. Besides, she didn't see any of the male reporters from the New York *Chronicle* putting themselves in danger for the sake of a scoop.

When the ground around her began to shake as

something enormous moved past the narrow opening of the alleyway, she wondered if she might have made too brash a decision. She looked up—and up—at what was coming her way. "I should have brought my wide-angle lens."

A line of military vehicles sped down Fifth Avenue in a hasty retreat, jeeps overloaded with anxious soldiers training their rifles behind them. Tanks clattered along the pavement, knocking parked cars aside as they fell back from the approaching menace.

Booming impacts followed them, each footfall a slow and inexorable thunderclap. Even at their top speed, the tanks and jeeps could never get out of the way in time.

With plodding movements, towering monstrosities stomped in lockstep through an abandoned intersection, looming as tall as the corner building. Hulking mechanical giants walked side by side down the streets of New York City, crushing everything in their path.

These robot monsters had arms and legs thicker than the girders that formed the tallest skyscrapers. Round swiveling joints marked what would have been elbows and knees. Each disklike hand bore three curved metal claws, a garden rake large enough to rip a furrow down the side of a battleship. Square torsos studded with rivets as large as manhole covers contained the mechanical systems, engines, and power generators. Each armored chest bore the sinister emblem of an iron-winged skull.

The heads of the robot monsters were shaped like heavy welding helmets. A single antenna rose from the right side of each helmet, and a broad bright panel of glowing glass served as the blazing wide eye of a cyclops.

Hiding in side streets, police trained their machine guns on the robot monsters. They fired in vain, a constant barrage of bullets that did nothing more than sketch bright sparks across the metal. The iron giants strode down the deserted city street, not intimidated, not even slowed by the gunfire. One huge foot came down on a squad car, flattening it into scrap metal as a policeman flung himself to the side.

Side by side, unstoppable, the robot monsters marched toward their unknown destination.

Scrambling from his ruined squad car, the disheveled police sergeant raced for a call box, shouting into a two-piece handset. "They've broken through the perimeter. Send reinforcements. Send us everything you've got!"

At command headquarters for New York City Defense Operations, a radio operator received the urgent call for help. At times such as these, the local military and the NYPD could not face the threat alone.

A flashing red light on the wall added urgency. The radio operator opened a scarlet three-ring binder, flipped tabs, and reached the relevant section. He'd done this before. Taking a deep breath, he grabbed his desktop microphone and broadcast on the necessary frequency. "Emergency protocol 90206. Calling Sky Captain! Come in, Sky Captain! Repeat, calling Sky Captain and the Flying Legion. Come in, Sky Captain."

Radio waves pulsed out from a special transmitting tower atop the Empire State Building. Amplifiers and booster stations received the signal and retransmitted it across the city, over the North American continent, the Atlantic Ocean, and across Europe. At the speed of light, the distress call crisscrossed the planet, summoning the brave aerial hero wherever he might be.

As the robot monsters lumbered ahead, the radio operator's voice continued to echo through the sky.

Then, from far out in the lower part of New York

Bay, racing in from the Atlantic and through the Hudson River Narrows, a rumbling roar cut like a sword through the thick cloud base. Superfast engines drove the plane forward like an angry hornet, between Staten Island and Brooklyn, then over Manhattan.

Bursting through the murk, a P-40 Warhawk swept in between the tall buildings, flying as if obstacles meant nothing. The ferocious fanged mouth of a snarling tiger was painted across the plane's nose behind the blurred circle of the furious propeller. A painted pair of glaring red eyes seemed to search for targets ahead. Three 20mm machine guns mounted in each wing extended forward, loaded and ready to fire upon the mechanical monsters.

Sky Captain had arrived. Wedged into the cockpit of the battle-worn fighter, Captain Joe Sullivan worked the controls as if they were extensions of his fingertips. He felt his plane and sensed its movements with an uncanny instinct.

The radio operator's static-laced voice came again through a tinny speaker in the headset: "Come in, Sky Captain. . . ."

With a gloved hand, Sky Captain raised his microphone and depressed the transmit key. The taciturn leader of the heroic Flying Legion was an aerial daredevil of unparalleled skill, and he radiated confidence as he roared toward the giant robot monsters. "This is Sky Captain. I'm on my way."

His leather hood fit snug against his hair, and goggles sat in place over his eyes. He hunched into the fleece-lined collar of his leather bomber jacket, ready to go.

The aluminum alloy propeller blades whirred like a buzz saw almost to invisibility. His P-40 did an arching loop as he rocketed toward the enormous robots menacing Manhattan.

*　　*　　*

Down in the chaotic streets, Polly was not about to let this story get past her. She skirted the abandoned police barricade and continued through the alleyway toward the other end. She dodged garbage cans and two empty boxes made of corrugated cardboard. Finally, she saw brighter light ahead, the last remnants of dusk. Automatic neon signs and streetlights began to glow as if it were any normal evening.

She made a run for the cross street, racing down the alley and into the wider avenue—emerging directly into the path of the marching robots.

In her sensible shoes, she slid to a stop in the middle of the street, craning her neck to stare. Her minuscule form was like a lone doll in front of the mammoth iron monsters crunching toward her down the street. She froze, knowing the robots must have seen her.

As the huge machines loomed over her, blazing cyclopean eyes cast harsh illumination down the evacuated street, as if scanning for something. Polly realized that if she could take this photograph, there was a Pulitzer Prize in it for certain.

In the middle of the street, Polly popped off the camera lens cap and determinedly advanced the film. Because her hands were trembling, she decided on a fast shutter speed, but with the fading daylight, maybe she did need a longer exposure. She raised the camera, pressed her eyelashes against the viewfinder, and lined the nearest robot monster in her sights. *Steady . . . steady.*

Before she could snap the photo, an enormous blast hit the side of an adjacent building, smashed by one of the destructive robots. The explosion sprayed rubble in all directions, and the shock wave threw Polly to the ground. Knocked from her hand, the camera skittered across the street to disappear into a drain gutter.

Polly jumped to her feet and raced for the gutter. The robots plodded forward, each massive footfall cracking the pavement. If she didn't hurry, she would either be squashed or lose her shot.

She dropped to the curb, not caring about the mud, dirt, and garbage. Urgently squeezing her hand through the sewer grating, she stretched her arm to its full length.

The ranks of giant robots marched ahead in lockstep. Their feet sounded like metal drumbeats shaking the ground. With her face close to the pavement, she stretched her arm down into the grate, and her fingers quested for the fallen camera. Her fingers tantalizingly touched the leather strap.

A dark shadow fell over her, cast by the oncoming machines. Polly looked up in terror to see the robot juggernauts only a few giant steps from her.

She tried to stay focused as her fingertips grazed the camera strap again, nudging it, until finally she touched the camera itself. She strained so hard she felt as if she were pulling her arm out of its socket. Then she slowly, carefully curled her pinky finger around the thin strap. Delicately, as if it were filled with nitroglycerine, she began to lift the camera out of the gutter.

Grinning in triumph, Polly pulled it out of the drain and jumped to her feet. Now that the camera was safe, she needed to get out alive.

She rushed toward the alley, but stopped short as the concussive force of the giant machines made the brick buildings shake and buckle. Chunks of concrete and mortar rained down on the street, blocking her way. Polly spun around, suddenly serious. She considered her options.

Farther down the street, the police had reassembled at a second fallback barricade. With pistols, rifles, and machine guns, they opened fire on the machines, unaware of her presence. Hot bullets ricocheted off the robots' bodies, singing and sparking in all directions.

Polly raced to the sidewalk, but buildings blocked

her path on either side. She could dodge the hulking machines more easily than she could stay out of the way of the hail of bullets. Chunks of debris continued to crash around her, creating a dusty haze. She could never make it back to the barricade and the dubious protection of the police.

Polly took a tentative step backward, her mind racing. Then, with a look of resolve, she reached down and ripped the side seam of her skirt, freeing her legs because she needed to run.

"Desperate situations sometimes call for crazy solutions," she said aloud. Editor Paley had told her that when she'd been a new reporter doing nothing more dangerous than covering social gatherings and orchid shows. At the time, he had been giving her only theoretical advice so that he could sound wise. The older man had never expected her to be in a situation where she could actually put the idea into practice. "So here's my crazy solution."

With only one way out, Polly took a deep breath— and then bolted directly toward the robots. The monstrosities were huge but slow, and she had plenty of room to move. It seemed like a workable idea, though she had to admit the situation looked worse and worse the closer she came to the machines. One giant foot came down with a thud.

The best thing about brash actions was that, once she decided upon them, she couldn't change her mind. Like an insect about to be crushed, Polly dodged between giant legs. She ducked as an arm the size of a construction crane swung over her with a rake of crowbar-thick claws. Then she swerved to the side as an enormous metal foot as big as a taxicab landed in front of her. The force of the stomping step was so great the aftershock knocked her to her knees.

She looked up at the upraised iron shoe descending only a few feet above her. Gasping, Polly rolled out of the way as the robot boot struck the pavement. Another foot crashed down next to her, followed by another and another, like mortar fire. Polly covered herself as the street was pounded on all sides.

The deafening, whirring noise of robot gears made Polly roll, turning to look up into a shadow. The heel of a raised metal boot hovered over her body. Polly watched, helpless and unable to scramble out of the way as the robot's foot started downward.

There was no escape. She was doomed.

episode 2

"WINGED TERROR"

After arriving in New York City aboard the *Hindenburg III*, Dr. Jorge Vargas has mysteriously vanished.

With the city helpless and under attack by giant mechanical monsters, a distress call is sent out to Sky Captain and the Flying Legion.

Meanwhile, Polly Perkins has fallen into the path of the hulking machines and is about to be crushed underfoot. . . .

6

To the Rescue
A Crater in Manhattan
A Worldwide Disaster

Only seconds from being crushed underfoot, Polly knocked her camera out of the way. It skittered aside, rattling on the pavement. Maybe at least the photos would be saved. Then, in dismay, she realized she hadn't managed to take any good shots yet. The robot's foot descended, and Polly knew exactly what a bug must feel like.

Suddenly, swooping down Fifth Avenue as if the tall skyscrapers created no obstacle at all, the P-40 Warhawk threw itself into the metal monster's path.

A volley of machine gun fire from all six of Sky Captain's wing cannons knocked the towering machine backward. Already off-balance with one leg upraised, the robot tottered, allowing Polly sufficient time to escape. She rolled away, breathless, pausing just long enough to snag her camera. As she ran, Polly raised her hand to throw Sky Captain a mock salute while he roared past. Then she scrambled for cover behind a pair of hastily erected sawhorses blocking a narrow alley.

The cheers of frightened policemen rang out from farther down Fifth Avenue, where another last-stand barricade had been erected. Sky Captain gained altitude above the tall buildings, banked his wings, and circled around for another pass against the robot giants.

At an intersection ahead, four of the clanking warriors had converged from different streets. Anchoring their feet, they turned glowing eye visors toward the ground, then unleashed dazzling white rays. The energy beams, all focused on the same section of pavement, shot out from the robot heads, gathering intensity as they overlapped.

Under the onslaught, the street began to bubble and crack. A fifth walking robot marched in beside the others and shot his own ray. Rubble exploded from the impact. The robots continued their eerie barrage, gouging a giant hole as if they were pirates with a treasure map and an "X" had been marked in the middle of Manhattan.

Coming in from behind the giant walking machines, Sky Captain unleashed another flurry of bullets. The hot lead hammered the helmeted heads like rivets flying from a manic construction worker, but the bullets did not slow the robots from continuing relentlessly forward.

The Warhawk sped between the ranks of machines, all of them sporting the winged-skull insignia. Sky Captain frowned, wondering what evil genius had created this army. Then he yanked the control stick, throwing his plane into a barrel roll to avoid an enormous slow-moving arm that swung across his path like the arm of a drunken giant who was swatting at a bee. The sharp banking maneuver knocked Sky Captain against the glass canopy of the cockpit, smacking his head hard. Sky Captain winced and pulled up, his engine howling. The robot's three hooked claws just missed his wing as he rocketed heavenward.

Undaunted, Sky Captain maneuvered his airplane through a narrow alleyway, easily threading the obstacle course as he cruised low. He banked left, then left again as he circled the block. Anxious for another crack at the tin-can monstrosities, he found an alley that would take him back where he needed to go. He dove down the narrow street—and then saw the black cables from a telephone pole looping from one building to another at the far end, crossing the alley opening like a spiderweb.

With no time to move, no room to dodge, Sky Captain took aim and fired a burst from his wing-mounted cannons. The spray of bullets riddled one of the telephone poles, splintering the thick wood like a wheat stalk severed by a scythe. As his Warhawk raced forward, the telephone poles tottered and fell forward, directly into the path of the lumbering robot giants.

The lead robot's legs became tangled in the sparking wire, its gears straining. As it stumbled, the other foot stepped on the rolling telephone pole, and the enormous mechanical monster lost its balance. With painful grace, the robot giant slowly began to topple.

The P-40 burst safely out of the alley and arced high. Sky Captain watched the huge walking monster fall.

On an earlier mission against the Rocket Robbers—villains who launched explosive missiles against armored bank buildings and then swooped into the rubble with jetpacks to steal gold bullion—one of the Flying Legion's heavy planes had been damaged. The brave pilot had barely been able to bring the large aircraft to the ground. Sky Captain had circled overhead, radioing advice and instructions, knowing the impact would be terrible. Leaking fuel, the heavy plane had crashed in Central Park like a blacksmith slamming a sledge into an anvil, the worst accident Sky Captain had ever witnessed. But when the robot monster smashed headlong into Fifth Avenue, the impact was far more spectacular.

The weight of the huge giant created a fissure that split open the pavement. The wide crack zigzagged up the street, directly between Polly's legs. She stood with her feet planted, her camera poised. As the action reached its crescendo, she clicked photo after photo, determined not to miss the shot this time. Then she stared directly in front of her, where the robot had collapsed only a few feet from her. Polly took a final picture, for good measure. One of them was sure to win a Pulitzer.

Suddenly, in the streets around her, everything stopped. The robot army paused. Sky Captain's plane raced away for another run, but the police ceased firing their machine guns. A breathless moment passed.

Strangest of all, the rows of giant robots stood frozen in the middle of the street. Beeping, chirping signals emanated from the antennae mounted to their blunt heads. The robots froze, as if listening to new instructions; then inexplicably, the mammoth walking army raised their metal arms in unison. With great blasts of rockets from their feet and the exhaust nozzles in their iron torsos, the huge machines lifted from the ground and flew skyward. From nearby streets, all the marching robots rose up like a flock of vultures taking wing.

As Sky Captain sped forward, prepared to launch another attack, the ascending robots cut upward into his path, and he had to dodge before his plane was smashed. The iron giants continued to rise in waves, until they were finally swallowed in the clouds as quickly as they had appeared. . . .

*   *   *

Cowed New Yorkers began to peep out of their air-raid shelters, venturing into the streets to stare in awe at the damage the mechanical monsters had caused. Crowds stood out in front of buildings, watching as Polly approached the fallen robot sprawled along Fifth Avenue. Curious onlookers pressed closer to the iron giant like Lilliputians encircling a sleeping Gulliver.

Polly snapped another photograph. Maybe Editor Paley would give her a raise.

Finally, the droning air-raid sirens fell silent. The squadrons of walking robots had departed. Emergency vehicles rolled into place: fire trucks, ambulances, police cars. But the focus of the outcry seemed even greater two blocks away, where the army of robots had been headed. Anxious to discover what could be more intriguing than the fallen mechanical monster, Polly hurried after the curiosity seekers.

Now she saw—but didn't understand—what the robot force had been trying to do. The huge machines had torn open a gigantic crater in the ground, a gaping hole in Midtown Manhattan. Stripping away the street, the robot monsters had exposed New York City's massive underground electrical generators, the turbines and pumps that powered the entire metropolis. It reminded Polly of surgeons making an incision preparatory to the removal of a vital organ from a patient.

"What were they doing?" she muttered aloud, but none of the pedestrians around her answered. Maybe the machines weren't finished yet.

Lifting her camera, Polly snapped a photo of the crater just as Sky Captain reappeared. His P-40 soared overhead as he made sure everyone down on the ground was all right. Polly turned, a thoughtful expression on her face as she watched the aerial hero race away from her—as he so often did.

*   *   *

Finally, she got the headline story for the extra edition of the *Chronicle*. Ninety-point type, huge bold sans serif letters screamed out what everybody in New York already knew: ⁻

MECHANICAL MONSTERS INVADE GOTHAM
by Polly Perkins

And there was one of her photographs, too. She had taken so many good pictures, Editor Paley devoted one entire interior page to a special photo insert. Though he had chastised her for risking her life so foolishly, as soon as she stepped out of his office and closed the door, she'd heard him yelling at the *Chronicle*'s other reporters because they hadn't demonstrated the guts that she had. "You all missed the story of the century!"

This was one time Polly went down to the plant and stood watching the printing presses. She lifted the first copy as it came down the line, scanned her byline to make sure nothing was misspelled, and strutted proudly back to her office.

Radios tuned to different stations broadcast continuing updates of the recent disaster. The news reports overlapped, but the severity of the situation was already clear. Manhattan had not been the only target, but merely one step in an overall plan.

". . . further details of the attack continue to pour in . . ."

". . . central portion of the city is blacked out from radio communication due to damaged power lines and electrical failure . . ."

". . . cables received from English, French, and German news agencies now confirm the attack was not limited to New York City . . ."

Assessing the scope of the robots' assaults, Polly

brought a detailed world atlas to her desk, moving her glowing globe desk lamp so that she could spread open the large book. "Sky Captain" Joe Sullivan had tackled the enormous robots single-handedly over Manhattan, but the rest of the mercenary Flying Legion had responded to other emergencies across the world.

Hulking mechanical men stalked through the streets of Paris, damaging the Eiffel Tower, stripping the skeletal structure of its steel girders. In London, ranks of the destructive robots plodded past Big Ben, smashing two bridges across the Thames. Even in Moscow, faced by new Soviet Army tanks constructed on orders from People's Chairman Molotov, the mechanical men smashed the Communist defenders and began to tear apart new industries, raiding them for raw materials and heavy equipment.

Darting attack planes from the Flying Legion had met with minimal success. The robots, seeming to come from nowhere, performed their tasks and swatted aside all attempts to stop them. Then the iron giants departed, leaving only scars and mysteries.

". . . the BBC is reporting that a steel mill in Nuremberg was virtually excavated by what witnesses describe as a mechanized tornado . . ."

". . . news agencies in Paris and Madrid speak of strange burrowing machines rising from the ground, robbing entire communities of their coal and oil reserves . . ."

The mad genius who had invented these things—perhaps the mysterious Totenkopf Dr. Jennings had warned her about—must have a detailed scheme in several phases. She hadn't been able to find Jennings after he'd fled Radio City Music Hall, and now Polly understood that he had good reason to fear for his life.

And what had happened to Dr. Jorge Vargas, who had disappeared after the *Hindenburg III* had docked?

It was all part of an overall scenario—she knew it. Resting her chin on one hand, she listened to the radio.

"Meanwhile, the world can only wait in wonder as government officials join with the mercenary forces of Sky Captain and the Flying Legion to uncover the meaning of these mysterious events. . . ."

7

A Hidden Base
Inspired by Scientifiction
A Robotic Specimen

Even if they hadn't exactly been defeated, the menace of the giant walking machines was gone from New York. Sky Captain left the city far behind, rocketing across water, across land, through splashes of cottony clouds. Finally, he sped toward a steep, mountainous rise in the distance.

By now, the rest of the Flying Legion should be returning from their missions around the world. In all his years of adventuring, Joe Sullivan couldn't ever remember receiving so many widely separated distress calls coming in at once. A good day's work for the world's heroes. Whoever had built those terror machines was going to be a big problem.

With engines purring along, the P-40 began to climb, following the contour of the mountains until a camouflaged valley came into view. Nestled inside a pocket of densely wooded hills, reachable only through a confusing maze of winding dirt roads—or of course from the air—lay a massive operation: the secret base of the famous Flying Legion.

Awesome silvery zeppelins were anchored to mooring posts that rose high over the installation. A flat expanse of tarmac covered most of the valley floor. Runways extended in several directions toward the wooded mountains, offering options for takeoff and landing runs. Rows of war-rated aircraft were stationed on painted lines, ready for deployment in any emergency. A series of gargantuan hangars were spaced across the landscape, full of machinery, maintenance equipment, testing bays, and crew quarters.

Sky Captain felt a shiver of pride each time he came home. The location of the base wasn't common knowledge, for security reasons—but he felt that if the crazed megalomaniacs could just see what they were up against, half of them wouldn't even bother trying to take over the world. That would certainly make his job easier. . . .

After a smooth landing, Sky Captain's Warhawk taxied down the airstrip, where he was met by his ground crew. Waving directions as they walked confidently backward, two crewmen guided his plane into one of the hangars. Inside the huge building, catwalks were strung like cobwebs from rafter to rafter. The maintenance team rushed forward to surround the Warhawk like a pit crew in a motorcar race.

Letting the engine idle loudly, Sky Captain slid open the plane's canopy. He had to yell over the noise. "She needs refueling—and freshen up the ammo on the wing cannons." He climbed out onto the wing spouting orders, as if his support people didn't know what they were doing.

"Right, Sky Captain."

"And check all the hoses for nicks. Plug up any bullet holes on the fuselage. The usual."

"Bullet holes? Did you get shot at, Cap? I thought you were up against giant robots—"

"*I* did the shooting, Jimmy. But with all that ammunition flying around, a few ricochets might've gotten me."

"We'll make her good as new, Cap."

"You always do." With an easy jump, he dropped to the sealed concrete floor of the hangar. He drew a deep breath, comforted by the smells of airplane fuel, hot exhaust, and engine grease.

"I want to get a look at the film from the forward cameras as soon as it's ready—those robot monsters were something else! And get me a duty log. I want all the Legion's squad leaders assembled in one hour. I'll brief them myself, and then I want to hear what they encountered out there." He wriggled out of his backpack. "Where's Dex?"

The nearest mechanic grinned. "Where else would he be, Cap?"

A colored comic panel torn from the Sunday edition of the New York *Chronicle* showed Buck Rogers in his futuristic outfit. While an alien villain held Wilma Deering hostage, Buck showed his stuff, intimidating the evil mastermind by pointing a ray gun at a steel wall. A text balloon read, "My sonic atomizer can slice through metal like a knife through butter."

The comic panel was taped to a drafting table with notes scribbled in the margin of the newsprint. Beside it, extensive blueprints showed detailed designs of a gadget that looked remarkably similar to Buck Rogers's sonic atomizer.

His brown eyes glittering with anticipation, Dex Dearborn—Sky Captain's right-hand man and technical genius—pointed his strange-looking pistol at the other side of the room. The ray gun had an aiming fin, colorful buttons, and a curved handle that looked like it was designed for an alien hand.

Dex wasn't sure if all the knobs and adjusting buttons were necessary, but he didn't want to second-guess the revered comic artist. As soon as he proved that the sonic atomizer worked, he could probably add other functions to correspond with the ornamental controls.

With the pink tip of his tongue protruding from the corner of his mouth, he aimed the nozzle of the ray gun at a thick vertical slab of steel inside a cement bunker. The ray gun felt tingly in his hand, as if anxious to prove itself. Glancing over his shoulder, Dex called to his assistants, "All clear!"

Lab workers scurried from the thick-walled bunker to duck behind sheltered barricades. Dex pulled a pair of tinted safety goggles over his eyes, aimed the nozzle toward the center of the target plate, and squeezed the firing button.

Concentric rings of light struck the metal slab. An impressive warbling crackle thrummed out of the gun. Pulse after pulse of light shimmered against the surface of the steel plate. In less than a second, the metal began to glow white-hot, vibrating as it melted.

Releasing the firing button, Dex lowered the ray gun, impressed. "Excellent power output! And the gun mechanism isn't even hot." He set the ray gun on the table and hurried up to the metal slab as his assistants crept from behind the barricades, wiping sweat from their foreheads. Dex admired the results of the test: a huge melted hole in the center of three-inch steel.

"That Buck Rogers knows his stuff!"

Behind him, the giant doors of the research hangar rattled open to flood the interior with sunlight. Dex turned from the melted target plate, listening to the bass rumble of a powerful truck engine outside. Two of his assistants yelped in alarm and stepped away from the yawning doors as a massive semitrailer backed up.

On the trailer bed rested a giant robot carcass, five stories tall. It was battered and scratched but intact. Its once-blazing eye plate was now dim; the cables and gears were frozen; the power generator stilled. Dex couldn't believe what he was seeing. His jaw dropped. "Shazam!" He absently rested his hand on the hot metal of the target plate, then snatched it away and sucked on his fingers.

Silhouetted by the sunlight, Sky Captain strode into the hangar, his leather jacket halfway unzipped, his aviator goggles perched on his forehead. The semi driver shouted, sticking his head out the window and looking for directions as two Legion crewmen guided the flatbed backward. The prone robot was hauled slowly through the yawning doors. The iron monstrosity barely fit inside.

"Hello, Dex. See what I tripped up in Manhattan? I thought you might like to tinker a bit."

Dex put his hands on his hips jokingly. "I heard you describe it over the radio, Cap. I thought you said this thing was *big*?" But he couldn't maintain his nonchalance as he walked in a daze to the robot's giant welder-helmet head. He was dwarfed by the size of the mechanical behemoth. "Can I have it?"

"You figure out where it came from, and I'll get you one for Christmas. Promise." If anybody could dismantle and understand the enormous machine, Dex could. As always, Sky Captain had complete faith in him.

As a young and starry-eyed dreamer, Dex had worked in a malt shop often frequented by members of the Flying Legion. He'd done well in school, but spent most of his time reading comic strips and pulp magazines, watching movie serials, and listening to radio adventures. He loved to imagine the impossible while paying little attention to the practical. His parents had despaired of their Dexter ever making anything of himself.

But he'd loved to jabber to Sky Captain and the heroic members of the Flying Legion. The most important question of his life was: *What if?*

Captain Joe Sullivan had seen the genius behind the

young man's enthusiasm. Dex truly believed in the possibilities and in himself—and so Sky Captain gave him a chance in the Flying Legion. He'd strutted into the malt shop one day, cocky and confident, and rested his elbows on the speckled counter. "If I give you all the resources and support you need, and you give me all your imagination and your best work, then I guess we'll be unstoppable. Right, Dex?"

Dex drew most of his inspiration from the "scientifiction" magazines he loved so much: *Amazing Stories*, *Wonder Stories*, *Astounding Science Fiction*, *Marvel Science Stories*, *Famous Fantastic Mysteries*, *Planet Stories*, and so many others he could barely keep up with them all. His favorite authors gave him all the ideas he could possibly need: Jack Williamson, Edmund Hamilton, E. E. "Doc" Smith, even Edgar Rice Burroughs and H. G. Wells.

Some of Dex's inventions had been rather spectacular failures, but more often than not an innovation of his had allowed the Flying Legion to save the world. The improvements he'd made to Sky Captain's P-40 Warhawk alone were tremendous. Overall, Dex was worth his weight in collectible pulp magazines.

"So, Dex, while the rest of the Legion's been off fighting mechanical monsters, what have you been doing here in your cozy research hangar? Any breakthroughs for me?" Sky Captain looked meaningfully at the new ray gun and the melted hole in the steel target plate.

Snapping out of his reverie, Dex gestured for him to follow. "That was a good test. The sonic atomizer shows a lot of potential. But there's something else you need to see."

He led the pilot around the workbench toward an oscilloscope, where he flipped a switch. He tapped the curved glass surface of the cathode ray tube, tracing a jagged radio signal that appeared on the screen. "I recorded this signal just before the first machines appeared in New York, Moscow, Paris, Madrid, London. I didn't think anything of it until I played it back, while you were chasing giant robots."

Dex twisted a dial on his console. A series of ominous, repeating tones came through a small speaker. It had a rhythm, almost a melody of electronic information. Sky Captain leaned closer to the oscilloscope as if it would help him concentrate on the tones. "Morse code?"

"That's what I thought at first, but the syntax is more complex. There's a subcarrier hidden in the lower frequency. I think it's being used to control them—all the machines, from a central place."

"If it shows up again can you track it?"

"I can try."

"Good boy, Dex." Pulling off his gloves, Sky Captain gestured to the enormous robot lying prone on the semitrailer. "In the meantime, see what you can do with that big lug. Find out what makes it tick." Sky Captain gave Dex a mischievous grin. "You don't mind, do you?"

Dex tried to suppress his glee. "I don't mind."

Sky Captain tossed his gloves onto the workbench as he moved toward an arching doorway. "I want to know where these robots came from, Dex. Who sent them here? I'll be in my office."

He didn't slow his stride as he walked into the Flying Legion's center of operations. Inside, the showpiece was a giant detailed map of the globe spanning four stories and taking up three walls of the research hangar. Uniformed technicians walked overhead on catwalks, using pointers and wooden sticks to mark regions on the map. A booming loudspeaker relayed new coordinates as other members of the Flying Legion reported in.

Sky Captain spared only a glance for the bustling

activity, though. He nodded to the crewmen, but he was intent on a doorway on the opposite side of the map room. He headed for his private sanctuary, the place where he could think best. The name in stenciled letters on the door read, CAPTAIN H. JOSEPH SULLIVAN.

Barely containing his sigh of relief, Sky Captain entered the dark office and closed the door behind him. After a brief pause, he turned his back and leaned wearily against the door. His posture changed, and he reached for his aching ribs, feeling with fingertips to discover just how badly he had been hurt. The battle against the robot monsters had taken its toll, but Sky Captain knew never to let the world, or even the rest of his crew, see him like this.

He walked gingerly through the tiny office to a small wooden desk and sat down, exhausted. Still in shadow, he opened a side drawer, pulled out a shot glass, and set it on the desk after sweeping file folders and paperwork aside. Sky Captain reached back into the deep drawer and withdrew a bottle: milk of magnesia. He poured a full shot of the chalky white liquid, raised it in silent salute, and grimaced in preparation before touching the small glass to his lips.

A woman's voice startled him. "Tummy ache?"

Sky Captain spun around, drawing his pistol with a smooth speed that would have made a cobra jealous. He aimed at the dark corner of the room from which Polly Perkins stepped into the light, smiling at him.

Though surprised, he recognized her instantly. At first he reacted with pleasure, but then his expression darkened. Old wounds started to surface.

"How you been, Joe? Miss me?"

8

A Blueprint from Totenkopf
A Warehouse of Sinister Prototypes
More Clues About Unit Eleven

"**W**ho let you in here?" Sky Captain was unable to keep the bitterness out of his voice. "Get out. Fat lot of good it does to have a hidden base if everybody, including annoying newspaper reporters, can just waltz in here."

"Nice to see you, too, Joe." She demurely sat on the corner of his desk. "Dex said you might be in a mood."

"Dex . . ." Gritting his teeth, he grabbed the black telephone receiver from his desk and dialed so roughly that he almost tore off the front of the phone. "Dex! Get in here!"

Polly shook her head, nonplussed. Her wavy golden hair was perfect. "It's been three years, Joe. Don't tell me you're still mad at me. I can't even remember what we were fighting about."

Moving as if he was imagining a stranglehold, Sky Captain set the phone back in its cradle. He turned to Polly with a slow burn, speaking so distinctly he bit each word as it came out of his mouth. "You. Sabotaged. My. *Plane!*"

"Right . . ." Polly said, her tone clearly saying the opposite. "Still suffering from delusions, I see."

"I spent six months in a Manchurian slave camp because of you." He looked away as the harsh memories flooded back. "They were going to cut off my fingers—"

Polly rolled her eyes; she'd heard this a million times before. "Joe, for the last time, I didn't sabotage your damn airplane."

"And it was all so you could get a picture of Tojo Hideki in his bathrobe! Of all the ridiculous reasons—"

She swung one leg over the other, relaxed. "You know, I'm starting to think you made up this whole 'sabotage' nonsense to cover up the fact you were cheating on me with your little mystery girl the whole time we were in Nanjing."

"Never happened. All in your imagination."

"Who was she, Joe? What was her name?"

Still angry, he said, "All right, her name started with an F. *Figment*. Figment O'Your Imagination. Now who's having delusions?"

Polly moved seductively toward Sky Captain at his desk, but he pulled back, raising his pistol again. "That's far enough."

"What are you going to do? Shoot me?" Polly batted her eyelashes.

The door swung open, and Dex hurried into the office. When he saw Sky Captain holding the gun on Polly, he grinned. "Great! You two made up. I knew you would."

Sky Captain stood from his desk chair, leaving the shot glass of milk of magnesia untouched. "This was a pleasure, Polly. Let's do it again in ten years. Dex, escort Miss Perkins off the base. If she resists, shoot her. And don't forget to clean up your mess afterward."

Dex looked at her shyly. "Hi, Polly."

"Hi, Dex."

The younger man's face flushed with embarrassment. "I . . . uh, I gotta . . ."

"I know, hon. It's okay." Lifting her chin and showing no loss of dignity at all, Polly let Dex escort her out of the office. Sky Captain followed them to the exit and prepared to give the door a satisfying slam.

Polly sniffed, then spoke loudly to Dex. "Just as well. I guess you wouldn't have been interested in *this* anyway." She dangled the strange schematic that Dr. Jennings had left in the theater.

Even with just a glance, Sky Captain could see that the blueprint showed the detailed workings of the giant robots that had menaced Manhattan. He released his death grip on the door handle, seething. "Where did you get that?"

Polly turned with a smug smile on her face. He reached for the blueprint, but she withdrew it. "Oh, there's more where this came from. A lot more."

"I want that blueprint, Polly. Uh . . . Dex needs it."

The younger man brightened. "Yeah, it would be useful."

"You want the blueprint, and I want this story, Joe. And you're going to help me get it."

Sky Captain took a deep breath. He would rather have been fighting any number of evil geniuses bent on exterminating humanity. Dex stood next to Polly, still grinning. "Hey, maybe we should show her, Cap. Maybe she can help."

A quick look from Sky Captain shut him up, but Polly saw it.

"Show me what?" She calmly folded the blueprint and stuffed it back in her bag, refusing to move farther from the office. "Show me *what*?"

Out in the bright sunlight, Dex, Polly, and Sky Captain stood at the entrance of one of the Legion's warehouses. After fumbling in his pocket, Dex produced a ring heavy with jingling keys. Though he had dozens to choose from, the younger man selected the proper key without pause, opened a padlock securing the warehouse, and slid open the tall corrugated door.

"Here we are, Polly. Wait till you see this." Dex flipped a switch, and the room lights shone down upon row after row of incredible scientific artifacts. "I always told Cap we should open a museum or something."

The warehouse held a bizarre collection of mechanical oddities: giant burrowing machines with tractor treads and jagged conical prows, clunkier models similar to the robot giants that had just attacked New York City, coffin-sized glass cylinders holding electrical creatures that swirled about like lighting in a bottle, flying contraptions that defied description.

Polly's jaw dropped. "My God, what is this? Where did they all come from? Dex, did you—"

The younger man blushed. "Oh, no, Polly. Even I don't have enough imagination to create designs like these."

She'd been following the exploits of Sky Captain and the Flying Legion for years now, and she knew most of the enemies they had fought. She remembered their battles with the Fossil: a man who, after injecting himself with Tyrannosaurus blood extracted from amber, was converted into an atavistic creature determined to bring back dinosaur rule. The Flying Legion had been severely damaged by the Fossil's pteranodon-style flying war vehicles.

And then there was the Lensmaster, who had used meteorite glass in a viewing scope that let him see into another, sidewise universe. The Lensmaster could step around the fabric of space, past the tightest security, to assassinate world leaders. When Sky Captain had finally cornered him, the Lensmaster fled through his scope and stumbled into an impossible dimension where he remained lost to this day. . . .

None of the contraptions, though, looked familiar to Polly.

"They started appearing three years ago—an invasion of innovative robotic designs, all of them obviously created by the same design team," Dex said. "We've managed to keep it secret until now."

Sky Captain didn't have much to say as Polly followed the two men down the center aisle of the warehouse. Every step revealed something new and incredible.

Dex continued. "These machines showed up without warning, took what they wanted, and disappeared without a trace. Just like the recent attacks." He sighed. "Three years, and we still can't explain what they want or who sent them here."

He led Polly past a row of damaged machines, then stopped at a fearsome-looking mechanical crab. "We found this one outside Buenos Aires on May fourth." He gestured to a machine that looked like a manta-ray hovercraft with dangling steel cables, each of which ended in hooklike pincers. "This one crashed fifteen miles from Vienna on June thirteenth."

"June thirteenth?" Polly's brow furrowed as thoughts began to click together.

"And this one came down in—"

"Hong Kong, right?" Polly was excited.

Sky Captain stopped short. "That's right. What aren't you telling us, Polly?"

"And it was July eighth," she said, "in the evening."

"How do you know this?" Sky Captain demanded.

Polly did her best to look down her nose at him. "If you'd read the *Chronicle*, Joe, you might have followed the stories I've written. Those are the same cities where the scientists disappeared, and on the same dates. It can't be a coincidence."

Dex shook his head. "Shazam! Not a chance, Cap. Can't be a coincidence."

Sky Captain leaned closer, tired of games. "What else do you know?"

In answer, Polly approached one of the stored machines. "If I'm right . . ." With her hand, she brushed off a layer of grime and dust to reveal an ominous, familiar crest in the form of an iron skull with metal wings. Her tone grew serious. "Dr. Vargas was the sixth scientist to vanish mysteriously. Then a man—another scientist—sent me a message and arranged to meet me at Radio City Music Hall today. He was terrified, said someone was coming for him. I asked him who he was so afraid of, and he repeated one name. *Totenkopf.* He nearly went white when he said it."

"Totenkopf? Who is he?" Dex peered closely at the malicious-looking skull.

Polly withdrew a German newspaper article from her bag. "Apparently, he's the invisible man. I went through every record in the library twice, looking for anything. Called every contact I have from Paris to Bangkok. This was all I could dig up."

She spread the article on a flat surface of the deactivated machine. A grainy old photograph showed a group of seven men in lab coats surrounded by complex but unrecognizable apparatus. "Herr Totenkopf ran some kind of secret sciences laboratory stationed in Berlin before the start of the Great War. Something called Einheit Elf or Unit Eleven."

Despite his annoyance with her, Sky Captain looked closely at the article, scanning the young faces of the Unit Eleven scientists. None of them looked familiar to him. He didn't want to admit that he couldn't read the German text of the newspaper clipping.

"Nobody really knows what Unit Eleven was doing," Polly explained, "but there were rumors that they were conducting inhuman surgical trials on prisoners, and the facility was ordered shut down. Totenkopf disappeared with his research. There's still an international warrant for his capture. It's been more than thirty years since anyone's spoken his name, until today."

"After all that time, what makes you think it's him?" Sky Captain asked.

She pointed to a small inset photograph in the newspaper. "Note the insignia he chose for the unit."

He could barely make out an iron skull with metal wings. "The scientist who came to see you . . . where is he now?"

Polly looked at Sky Captain, a coy smile on her face. She dangled her information in front of him like a carrot on a stick. "So we're in this together . . . right, Joe?"

He stared her down, first scowling, then frowning in resignation as he knew she'd beaten him. "Polly, none of this gets published until I say so. You don't write a sentence or take a picture without asking me first. Understood?"

She nodded with solemn agreement. "Understood."

When he wasn't looking, Polly shifted the small camera under her arm. She stealthily snapped a picture of one of the giant machines in the museum warehouse.

9

An Important Address
An Intruder in the Laboratory
A Dire Warning

That afternoon, Polly's black Packard sped down a rain-soaked New York street, but it wasn't clear that she knew where she was going. Sky Captain sat sullenly next to her, staring straight ahead as she drove. He would have felt safer in the cockpit of his Warhawk, where at least *he* could have his hands on the controls.

When he sensed Polly starting to smile at him, he grew annoyed. He refused to look anywhere but through the wet windshield at the street. Finally, exasperated with the waiting, he said, "What?"

"I missed you, Joe." When he turned to look at her in surprise, she said, "Thanks for saving my life during the robot attack, by the way. If it wasn't for you, I would have ended up as a smear on the bottom of a big mechanical boot."

"Oh? Were you down there?" Sky Captain turned to the side and concentrated on counting brownstone doorways, lampposts, traffic lights—anything to maintain his feigned uninterest. "I didn't notice."

Polly continued to smile, not buying it. "I see you missed me, too. How nice."

"Mind the road." He leaned closer to the rain-streaked windshield, trying to see where they were going.

She slowed to a stop in front of a dark tenement building. "This is it, where Jennings is hiding—if my guess is right."

Leaving the car parked at the curb, Polly and Sky Captain hurried down the sidewalk. The leather bomber jacket kept him dry, but the cold sleet quickly matted his short brown hair. Polly wore a tan trench coat and a black fedora pulled low. He remained close at her side, not wanting to appear to be following her lead, as they turned the corner into a darkened alley. They descended a set of leaf-strewn stairs, past a junk pile of debris at one corner of the landing, to the door of a basement shop. A small placard read: ALLIED CHEMICAL.

After comparing the address to a scrap of paper in her hand, Polly knocked briskly at the door, but no answer came. "Hello? Dr. Jennings, it's Polly Perkins." She waited again, then knocked harder on the door. "Dr. Jennings?"

She flashed Sky Captain a worried look, and he reached for the doorknob, rattling it. "It's locked." Looking around for another way in, he spied an open window above them on the second floor. "See that window—there . . . ?"

He began to concoct an elaborate plan to gain entry. In the junk pile on the landing, he found a length of old rope coiled around two sagging boxes and a broken chair. He untangled the muddy strand so he could tie a loop in one end. He pulled hard to test the strength of the rope, hoping the fibers weren't too rotted. "We might be able to get in through that window if I can attach a line."

He heard a crash for his answer, and he looked to see Polly holding a rock in her hand. She smashed the door's window glass a second time, knocking the sharp splinters from the frame.

She dropped the rock, reached inside, and unlocked the door. "Never mind, Joe. It's open."

Sky Captain looked at Polly, his throat so full of conflicting words that he couldn't say any of them. Finally, he just brushed past her and pushed the door wide enough for them both to enter Dr. Jennings's lab. "I've seen my share of mad scientists and their laboratories. Usually they're better housekeepers than this."

The small lab had been thoroughly ransacked. File cabinets were yanked open, drawers emptied. Papers lay strewn all over the floor and on the overturned furniture. Broken test tubes and glass beakers littered the ground in puddles of colored, foul-smelling liquids. An off-kilter lamp lay sprawled against a wall; a writing desk had been smashed.

"We're too late," Polly said.

The two moved deeper inside, crunching through the debris. In the yellowish light of the dim lamp, Polly spotted a heavy metal cabinet in a far corner. Because iron brackets anchored the cabinet to the wall and floor, the vandals had been unable to tip it over. The latch to the cabinet had been broken.

Without telling Sky Captain what she intended to do, Polly strode directly to the cabinet and pulled open one of the loose doors. She blinked in disbelief, then raised her camera.

The cabinet held shelf upon shelf of glass jars. Tiny skeletons floated in embalming fluid, showing alien body shapes she had never seen before. "Looks like the remnants of aborted experiments."

Then she saw something move, barely more than a shadow at the bottom of the cabinet. On the lowest shelf, Polly found another glass container—that one holding a live specimen. She couldn't believe her eyes:

a living, breathing elephant no larger than a bar of soap drank from a miniaturized trough. It lifted its trunk and let out a tinny bellow, like a child tooting a plastic whistle.

Beside her, Sky Captain knelt to stare at the tiny creature. He turned to her as if she was somehow to blame. "All right, Polly—no more games. Tell me what the hell is going on."

She shrugged. "I was hoping you could tell me. Dr. Jennings wasn't very talkative during our brief interview."

As the miniature elephant paced inside its doll-sized cage, Polly's eyes moved upward, hungry for explanations. She screamed and immediately regretted having done it in front of Sky Captain.

A man emerged from a hiding place among the ransacked furniture, staggering forward. He was much more haggard-looking than she had seen him in Radio City Music Hall. "It's Jennings!"

The scientist had a dazed look on his face as he stumbled toward them, his hands outstretched in a wordless plea. Sky Captain reacted quickly as Jennings collapsed into his arms. "Got you!"

He eased the scientist down to the cluttered floor, turning the other man's body to reveal a knife buried deep between his shoulder blades. Thick, fresh blood soaked the woolen fabric of his brown suit. His gold-rimmed glasses were askew on his pasty face.

Dr. Jennings looked up, struggling to speak. With one hand, he clutched the zipper of the pilot's leather jacket. His voice was weak, barely audible. "You must stop him. . . ."

Sky Captain and Polly froze as they heard a stealthy noise in an upstairs room. Letting Polly support the dying scientist's head and shoulders, Sky Captain got back to his feet but remained in a wary crouch. "Stay here. Maybe we're not too late after all."

Someone was moving quickly in the other room. He heard the sound of a window opening, the scrape of a wooden frame moving in the sash. He ran up the staircase and through the door into a smaller office. He arrived just in time to see the blur of a black-garbed figure climbing out the open window.

"Stop!" Sky Captain lunged to grab the shadowy figure by the arm. With a vicious tug on the fabric sleeve, he spun the stranger around and found himself face-to-face with a stunning woman. Her face was perfect, her lips a dark ruby red. Her eyes were covered by large, round glasses with opaque lenses. It didn't seem possible that she could see through them.

She wasn't what Sky Captain had expected at all. He loosed his grip, surprised. "Listen, I don't want to hurt you—"

The dark woman moved with unbelievable speed, striking him with a backhand that had the force of a catapult. The blow knocked him against the wall, cracking plaster. Reeling, he slid to the floor, his legs turning into noodles. Sky Captain grabbed the back of his head and silently mouthed, "Owww."

Before he could scramble to his feet, the strange and murderous woman leaped to the window again. Ignoring the hammers inside his skull, Sky Captain dove after her, managing to catch her wrist just as she jumped. His hand accidentally hit the window latch, which caused the window to drop with a thud. The pane of glass shattered, and he was forced to let go, ducking to avoid the flying shards. "Damn!"

Anxious, he leaned through the empty frame. The black-swathed woman landed with uncanny grace in the alleyway below, bent her knees for the briefest pause, then sprinted with lightning speed around the corner. She was gone in a flash.

With a disappointed sigh, Sky Captain withdrew from the window. "What the hell is going on?" He wondered what excuse he could tell Polly. His head still throbbed, and he could feel a few cuts on his face from the glass splinters.

Before he left the office, he noticed a leather satchel lying on the floor, as if it had been tossed under a writing table. Curious, he picked it up. This could be something. . . .

In the cluttered laboratory room, Polly knelt over Dr. Jennings, trying to comfort him, but she could see he was dying. He had lost too much blood already, and the knife wound was deep. With his failing strength, the scientist struggled to speak. "Miss Perkins . . ."

"I'm here, Doctor. I tracked you down."

"If Totenkopf finds them . . . nothing will be able to stop him. Nothing . . ."

Polly leaned closer to hear his faint words. "Finds what?"

Jennings squirmed to reach inside the pocket of his jacket with a bloodied hand, then removed two small test tubes. "Once he gets these . . . the countdown will start."

"The countdown for what?"

"This world . . . will end." Before he could say anything more, before Polly could grasp the magnitude of what he had said, the scientist wheezed out his last rattling breath and died.

"Dr. Jennings!" She tried to revive him, but it was no use. Polly gently pried the two test tubes from the scientist's hand and held them up. "The end of the world? In here?" Dumbfounded, she glanced up as Sky Captain reentered and knelt down beside her. "He's dead." With sluggish movements, Polly covered the body with a jacket.

"Well, the murderer got away . . . but I think I found something." Sky Captain held out the satchel.

Polly recognized it immediately. "Dr. Jennings had that case with him at the theater yesterday, just before the robots attacked." She took the satchel from him eagerly, even as she discreetly pocketed the test tubes. She decided to keep them hidden. Sky Captain didn't need to know everything—not yet.

As he watched, Polly unfastened the satchel's catch. Inside, she found a stack of papers. Her brows knitted as she leafed through them, understanding only snippets. "They're in German."

"We can translate them. At least five members of the Flying Legion—"

Suddenly the frightening wail of air-raid sirens filled the air for the second time in as many days. The bone-rattling tone echoed off houses and buildings. In the neighborhood, some residents frantically switched on lights, while others did exactly the opposite.

"Not again!" Polly said as she and Sky Captain raced to the laboratory window, looking up as searchlights crisscrossed the cloudy sky. They could both hear an ominous droning sound in the distance. Something powerful was approaching fast.

"I have to get back to the base," Sky Captain said.

Forced to leave the dead scientist behind, Polly grabbed the satchel and stuffed the papers inside. "I'm coming with you, Joe."

10

The Fearful Flying Wings
An Unwelcome Passenger
A Signal Located

Back at the Flying Legion's base in the distant hills, Polly's Packard roared onto the airstrip, covered with mud from skidding along the dirt roads. Before she screeched to a complete stop, Sky Captain had already jumped out of the car.

Receiving the alert signal even before New York's air-raid sirens activated, his flight crew had prepped the P-40 Warhawk. They sprinted along with him to the waiting airplane. "Didn't have time to touch up the paint job on the nose, Cap. Sorry. Looks like one of the painted fangs is chipped."

"At least tell me you fueled her up and reloaded the ammo."

The crewman impatiently rolled his eyes. "Of course we did *that*, Cap!"

On the airstrips, other planes thrummed, their props spinning, engines warming up. Several members of the Flying Legion had taken off and now patrolled the skies. The surveillance zeppelins lifted higher on their tethers.

Sky Captain shouted questions as he ran, leaving Polly behind. He did not want to be at the tail end of the other mercenary fighters. "So what is it? What's happening up there?"

"Reconnaissance picked up something on radar traveling at over five hundred knots—and coming straight for us."

"How soon before it gets here?"

Suddenly, in the sky above, a dozen shapes emerged from the sunset-tinged clouds. The crewman pointed upward. "Right about now, I'd say, Cap." Slanted daylight splashed across the sleek metal hulls of flying craft that looked like mechanical vultures.

Obscured by a rippling haze of air distortion, the shapes took on the form of giant silver bats. Perfectly streamlined, as if made of quicksilver, the graceful yet deadly flyers flapped long and narrow wings like mechanized pterodactyls. They made a shrill whistling sound like a pipe sliding through a metal sleeve. The enemy Flying Wings dove forward, blunt noses marred by clusters of 50mm cannons. The black gun barrels extended, then began to spit fire.

Sky Captain scrambled for his plane, stepping up onto the wing and sliding the cockpit canopy aside. "Time to get going! Remove the wheel blocks."

The enemy wings swooped down like hawks upon the Legion's airfield. Crewmen ran for shelter into the hangars. Two of the Legion's warplanes screamed down runways and took off. Swooping along with mechanical grace, the fearful enemy flyers spat out heavy machine gun fire. The ammunition struck home in a searing hailstorm that blew up a row of unoccupied aircraft parked on the field. As the Flying Wings rose upward again with an eerie whistle, they left a firestorm in their wake. Row after row of Legion airplanes detonated after the strafing barrage.

"Does everybody know where our secret base is?" Sky Captain muttered as he swung himself into the Warhawk's cockpit. He raced through the takeoff checklist, glancing at the dials and controls as he fastened his helmet and seated his goggles over his eyes.

"Wait a minute, Joe."

As the enemy Flying Wings raced past for another attack, engaging the Legion fighters already in the air, Sky Captain looked down in astonishment to see Polly climbing the narrow fuselage ladder up after him. "What are you doing?" He had to shout over the deafening roar of the P-40's engine.

"I'm coming with you!" Another volley of explosions ripped through one of the supply hangars, igniting barrels of aircraft fuel.

"Don't be stupid, Polly. Remember what happened the last time you flew with me?" The chaos and noise all around them made it impossible for him to manage a reasonable tone.

"We had a deal!" She didn't even slow, but kept climbing.

"This isn't a game, Polly. People are going to die! In fact, some of my best men probably already have."

Determined and beautiful, Polly refused to let go of the rungs, even though the airfield was exploding around her. Howling alarms and roaring engines increased the racket during the bombardment. "You're not leaving without me, Joe! Not this time! It's my story."

Sky Captain curled his gloved fist, anxious to go and considering just how much more time Polly could waste with her incessant arguing.

Wings flapping briskly, the alien-looking machines circled around and struck again and again until they succeeded in blowing up the main hangar from which the P-40 had just emerged. Ducking from the backwash of the explosion, he shielded his head from the debris and shrapnel pelting all around them. The tiny impacts on his plane's fuselage sounded like a hailstorm on a metal roof.

Like a swarm of alloy-plated bats, even more of the Flying Wings converged on the Legion's hidden base. Sky Captain gritted his teeth, fuming. *No time to argue.* "Get in!"

Polly scrambled up behind him and threw herself into the cockpit's backseat. Sky Captain didn't waste even a second checking on her as he slid the canopy shut. The Warhawk's engine seemed to be screaming a challenge as he accelerated forward, taxiing down the nearest runway.

In the sheltered map room, Dex sprinted toward a massive, blinking communications array. He pushed past several of the radio operators who were frantically trying to coordinate the defense of the base. Taking control, Dex began to flip a series of buttons, causing a jagged signal to appear on another oscilloscope display. He stared at the bouncing radio signal expectantly, adjusting dials to triangulate. An oddly melodic Morse code tone came through the small speaker, sounding similar to what he had heard earlier—only closer.

"There you are!" Dex made a victory fist. "This'll do it!" He grabbed a headset microphone from one of the pasty-faced radio operators and hurriedly spoke into it. "Cap, do you read me?"

The sounds of emergency sirens and explosions continued in the background. The lights dimmed briefly from the attack going on outside. It was only a matter of time before the Flying Wings leveled the control hangar—if Sky Captain didn't stop them first.

The Warhawk streaked through the sky in fast pursuit of three Flying Wings. Like superfast metal vultures, the enemy aircraft flapped furiously, pumping with pistons and powerful whistling engines. They wheeled and evaded, reminding Sky Captain of crows on the wing.

"Dodge all you want," he muttered, forgetting that Polly was sitting behind him, "but you can't outrun this." He lined up the nearest quicksilver machine in his crosshairs. His finger hovered over the trigger on his flight stick.

A voice burst over the radio set. "Cap, this is Dex! Come in!"

He lifted his microphone. "Hang on, Dex. I'm a little busy."

Sky Captain locked his sights on one of the machines. His gloved finger flipped open the safety latch on his trigger, and with complete coolness he squeezed. A stream of machine gun fire embroidered with intermittent tracers stitched across the sky, intersecting the Flying Wing. Gunfire penetrated the smooth quicksilver hull, making the enemy craft explode in a massive fireball.

With a satisfied sigh, Sky Captain lifted his microphone. "Go ahead, Dex."

"Whatever you do, Cap, don't shoot!"

Sky Captain frowned sheepishly at the expanding cloud of smoke and tumbling shrapnel that had been the Flying Wing. "Uh, okay."

Dex sounded disappointed. "You shot it, didn't you?"

"Yeah. I thought that was the point."

"Listen, Cap, you asked me to track down the command signal, and I did. The signal is coming from one of those machines. It must be the leader. You've got to keep them in one piece, or I'll never be able to get to the bottom of this."

Sky Captain groaned, but he had never found reason to disbelieve Dex. "You sure know how to make a job harder, Dex. Which machine is it?" Ahead of him and all around the smoldering Flying Legion base, dozens of the flapping aircraft swooped and dove, continuing their attack.

Dex did not sound reassuring over the radio set.

"No way of telling. It could be any one of them. Wait. . . . I'm losing the signal." The younger man groaned. "Now it's getting fainter."

Sky Captain saw that one of the Flying Wings had veered off from the others and headed back toward the New York skyline. The rest of the mechanical attackers concentrated their firepower on the hangars and runways below. "I think I found it, Dex. It's heading for the city."

"Don't let him get away, Cap!"

Sky Captain hated to leave the rest of the Legion to the greater battle, but he knew he needed to win the war against this sinister enemy. "You better be right, Dex."

"Keep after it! I need you to bounce that signal back to me. If we lose it now, we may never get it back."

With a heavy heart, Sky Captain raced after the primary Flying Wing. "Just let me know when you've got something, Dex. The very instant you have it."

"I'll let you know. Out!"

While Polly clutched her seat in the back of the cockpit, Sky Captain veered off in pursuit of the lone enemy craft racing back toward Manhattan.

11

A Dogfight over Manhattan
Thieves from the Sky
Polly's Shortcut

Inside the map room, Dex unrolled a large chart across the main table. He didn't even flinch as a nearby detonation rocked the Legion's control center. Oily smoke began to fill the hangar, and the lights flickered again.

Undaunted, Dex unwrapped a wad of bubble gum and popped it into his mouth. Debris sifted from above like a fine rain. Overhead, the Flying Wings continued to bombard the base, while brave Legion fighters mounted their best defense.

Dex yelled to the communications operators beside him. "I want a full-spectrum sweep of every incoming signal."

Two men huddled under tables for shelter from falling chunks of the roof, while other grim operators went about their duties, hunched over dials and transmitters. A Legion warplane zoomed overhead, unleashing a crackle of machine gun fire.

"Amplify any variant frequency cycle and route it to me!" Dex bent over the screen, staring so hard his eyes hurt, *willing* the answer to come in time to save Sky Captain and drive off the attack on the base.

Explosions continued outside. Orange-and-black fireballs spewed upward from destroyed planes on the runways. The attacking Wings targeted the tethered observation zeppelins. Though soldiers fired their rifles from the ground and warplanes dove in to protect the lighter-than-air vessels, they could not drive the Flying Wings from the dirigibles.

Incendiary projectiles tore through the thick fabric hulls, igniting the volatile hydrogen inside. Like the tragic end of the first *Hindenburg*, the Legion's zeppelins were engulfed in an inferno. Their blackened skeletons collapsed with slow grace to the tarmac as ground personnel fled.

Legion planes continued to attack the Flying Wings. A volley of vengeful shots sheared off the razor-thin wing of an enemy aircraft, and the quicksilver batlike form scraped across the main hangar's roof, showering sparks. It tumbled into a heap of wreckage on the tarmac outside the tall doors.

Inside the control hangar, Dex allowed nothing to break his concentration.

Streaking above the terrain on their way to New York City, Sky Captain kept his P-40 close behind the primary Flying Wing. The enemy craft flapped its powerful metal wings like a hawk swooping in for the kill.

They sped along the spine of Long Island, covering distance at an insane speed. The flight path of the fleeing attacker took them over Queens and the site of the soon-to-open 1939 World's Fair, billed as the largest international exhibition in history. Sky Captain looked down at the distinctive Trylon, a seven-hundred-foot-tall obelisk pointing toward the sky, and the two-hundred-foot globe of the Perisphere. President Roosevelt himself would give the kickoff speech, "Building the World of Tomorrow."

First, though, Sky Captain had to save the world of *today*.

The speeding aircraft crossed the East River in a flash, diving toward Midtown Manhattan. "If that Flying Wing thinks he can lose me among the skyscrapers, we'll see just who's better in an obstacle course."

"It's sweet, but you don't have to show off for me, Joe," Polly said from the rear of the cockpit.

He banked hard, barely keeping his annoyance in check. "I have absolutely no intention of showing off for you."

Weaving an erratic course, the Flying Wing dipped among the tall buildings, diving to street level, where taxicabs and buses swerved to avoid a collision. Sky Captain clung like glue to the enemy's exhaust.

Pulling up in a steep climb, they shot above the rooftops. Polly peered out the cockpit canopy, surprised to see six more Flying Wings engaged in furious activity below them. "Joe, there's another half dozen of them!"

He looked from side to side, but the goggles blocked his peripheral view. "Are they after us?"

She saw, though, that the six new enemy craft had taken up positions over the yawning crater the robot monsters had blasted the day before. Like a giant open wound, the city's heavy power generators lay exposed to the air.

"Not after us, Joe. Look what they're doing!"

The six Flying Wings had lowered giant cables, slowly extending the lines into the crater. Automatic clamps attached to the shafts and supports that held the huge turbines in place. Sparks flew, metal groaned, and finally the machinery was uprooted. Up and down the streets of Manhattan, windows and lighted neon signs went dark.

"They're taking the city's generators." Polly was genuinely puzzled. "Totenkopf is building something, and whatever it is needs enough power to light up a city."

Suddenly, three more Flying Wings descended upon Sky Captain's P-40, like owls intent on grabbing field mice. Quad clusters of wing cannons extended from the quicksilver bodies and opened fire. Bullets whizzed by, peppering the Warhawk's fuselage.

"They're just trying to distract me." Sky Captain hunched over the cockpit controls. He didn't take his eyes from the darting course of the primary Wing. "But it's not going to work."

"I think they're trying to *destroy* us, Joe, not distract us."

He didn't listen to her. The primary Wing plunged low, skimming car tops in its attempt to shake Sky Captain's plane. Pedestrians ducked or dove to the pavement.

Maintaining his reckless acceleration, Sky Captain roared after his prey. More bullets flew by from the Flying Wings behind them, shattering streetlamps and pocking building walls as the Warhawk soared down the narrow street.

Sky Captain called back to Polly, "You okay?"

"Great," she said, barely able to talk.

"There's a bottle of milk of magnesia under the seat if you need it. Sometimes amateurs get a bit airsick."

"I'm fine."

Sky Captain turned around, giving her a skeptical look through his goggles. "You don't look so good."

"Neither do you," Polly said, then her face froze. "Pull up!"

Sky Captain whipped his attention forward just in time to see a looming concrete-and-steel skyscraper directly in their path. Reacting instantly, he yanked on the flight stick so hard he feared he might rip it from the yoke.

Dex had made modifications to the P-40's engines,

its flaps, its air rudder, and now the plane responded like a dream. In a tight curve, the nose tilted immediately upward, and Sky Captain shot in a straight vertical so close to the skyscraper's wall that if he'd had his landing gear down, he could have left skid marks on the windows. The plane leaped over the building top, and before Sky Captain could catch his breath, he spotted the primary Wing again and set off after it.

The fleeing enemy aircraft headed straight for a billboard in a suicidal plunge. As it approached, staccato machine gun fire blasted the billboard's left support post. The wide rectangular sign tipped and slumped, lopsided, in a slow-motion fall. The enemy flyer ducked under the sign, wings pumping, and Sky Captain plunged after it. The billboard fell forward into their path.

"Joe!" Polly shouted.

"I see it. Too big not to notice." He yanked the stick, and the plane took a sharp turn, narrowly avoiding the crashing billboard. In the back of the cockpit, Polly hung on for her life as the plane rolled sideways and streaked down a cross street.

"Sorry to bother you, Cap," Dex said over the radio, "but I lost the signal."

"I'll find him, Dex. Sit tight."

Pressing her face to the cockpit window, Polly recognized where they were. "Oh! Turn left!"

"Sit back, Polly. Let me do the flying."

"There's a shortcut down Montgomery Street. You can catch him on the Third Street thoroughfare."

Sky Captain pointedly ignored her, continuing along his own chosen path. Polly leaned forward, shouting in his ear. "Listen to me, Joe. I know these streets like the back of my hand."

He glanced at her, reluctantly considering. She met his eye, insistent. *"Left."*

Sky Captain gritted his teeth and banked the Warhawk hard left, swooping low to avoid cables strung from rooftops. He realized too late that he had turned down a one-way street. The plane hurtled directly toward an oncoming gravel truck. The driver blared his horn, and Sky Captain pulled up, gaining a few feet of altitude to avoid hitting the truck. A stream of cars headed their way, swerving frantically, honking in alarm, smashing bumpers.

While wrestling to maintain control, he shot Polly an annoyed glance, but she didn't seem to be bothered. "Okay, keep on straight. . . . Wait! Go right."

"When?"

Her outstretched finger traced a line on the canopy glass, following the street they were already passing. "Back there."

He tensed his arms and shoulders, but pulled back on the flight stick, throwing the plane in a tight arc. He narrowly missed the side of a building. A thin clothesline snapped, and white garments fluttered to the ground. "I could use a little warning next time."

"Left!"

He yanked the flight stick again, and the Warhawk groaned in protest. Accelerating to make the course adjustment, Sky Captain nearly crashed into an oncoming building, squeaking past an extended flagpole.

"Damn it, Polly!" He looked behind them as the pursuing Flying Wings dove through the gap between tall buildings, closing in. Sky Captain opened the throttle, and the needle on the speedometer gauge climbed to two hundred miles per hour.

"Now left again." Polly's voice remained unflustered, as if she were simply giving directions to a garden party.

Grumbling, Sky Captain followed her instructions, cruising low to the busy street. Straight ahead, two oncoming cars split in a Y around his diving plane, just missing it. He wiped sweat from his forehead above his goggles.

Peering through the canopy, Polly said, "Left."

"No, we already crossed Third. We're going in circles."

"For once in your life, will you trust me? Left!"

Sky Captain swerved and suddenly found himself flying directly toward an elevated train. He dove at the last moment, avoiding the rattling train, but then he was heading straight into the path of two Flying Wings. Their quad-clustered machine guns opened fire.

He made a hard turn as the Warhawk arced all the way from the right lane across traffic to a perpendicular street. Strafing fire narrowly missed him, but now the enemy Wings settled close on their tail.

"Right!" said Polly.

He twisted the flight stick, veering them into another street.

"Left."

The plane scraped the edge of a building. "You're cutting it pretty close, Polly. Do you really know where we're going?"

They shuttled through a tight alley then emerged like a cannonball. Polly gasped, making a snap decision. "Right! It's here. Turn right!"

Another swift turn, and Sky Captain's eyes became huge as he realized they were not headed down an open avenue, but straight into the steel skeleton of a high-rise under construction. "It's a dead end. Some shortcut!"

More Flying Wings descended from above, blocking their path and forcing them toward the steel structure. The city was always growing, always expanding, always under construction. "That's . . . not supposed to be there," she said.

"I should strangle you, Polly, but I don't have the time right now."

Now that the Flying Wings converged closer, bullets hit the plane, some penetrating the special fuselage armor Dex had designed. A stray projectile found the fuel line, and high-octane aircraft fuel began to spray out.

"Oh, lovely." Fighting to keep control of the P-40, Sky Captain steered toward a small opening in the patchwork of girders in front of them.

Hard-hatted steel workers standing on the girders looked up in disbelief as the Warhawk flew straight toward them. They leaped out of the way, jumping for scaffolds, dangling from platforms as Sky Captain's plane entered the building at full speed. His wing glanced the edge of a girder, producing a trail of sparks as he soared forward. "Plenty of room."

As the pursuers reached the face of the building framework, they scattered in all directions, unable to follow.

Inside the skeletal building, not daring to slow his speed in the hollow labyrinth, Sky Captain fought to keep the plane steady as his wings nicked support beams that threatened to throw him into a spin.

He yelped as a swinging girder was slowly lifted into place in front of him, blocking their path. With no time or room to dodge, Sky Captain unleashed a burst from his wing cannons, aiming at the chain support. Sparks flew as the steel links split. The girder fell, clearing a path at the last possible moment, and the plane shot out of the cavernous building and into the open air again.

But only for an instant. Sky Captain saw the facing building just across the street. He knew he was flying much too fast to make the turn. He had one desperate chance. He grabbed for a newly installed lever in the control panel. He knew full well about the note taped to the lever:

Don't touch!
Dex

He yanked the lever anyway. A panel dropped open in the Warhawk's belly, and a sharp grappling hook shot out, dangling behind them on a reinforced cable.

With a clang, the hook wrapped around one of the exterior girders of the building framework. Suddenly anchored like a ball on a string, the plane swung about with its own momentum, making an impossible turn. The grappling hook disengaged at the end of the spin, dropping away.

Sky Captain didn't breathe. Nearly crushed by centrifugal force, he held on as his plane just cleared the building. It nicked a lighted theater marquee, popping a string of decorative bulbs. The sparking explosions ignited the gasoline dripping from the leaky fuel line. Fire began to lick up along the tube.

Polly stared out the window, too stunned to show any panic or excitement. She observed the burning plane matter-of-factly. "Joe . . ."

"I know, Polly. I know."

Tracking him down from a web of side streets and avenues, the full squadron of Flying Wings suddenly appeared. Gunfire flickered from their wing cannons.

Sky Captain swerved to avoid another skyscraper, then began to climb to rooftop level as his plane trailed smoke. Time for another crazy plan. Atop the towering buildings, he spotted what he had expected: a pair of mammoth water towers, cisterns stored for emergency consumption.

"Hang on." He shot at the nearest water tower, splintering its wood-slat side. Water streamed out, and Sky Captain flew straight for the gushing fountain, ducking into the spray. The sudden drenching doused the flames on his fuel line. He soared onward as water splashed away from his windshield and his wings.

Sharp silver wings pumping in pursuit, the enemy aircraft followed closely behind them. The plane streaked along the contour of the rooftop, past a giant motorized sign, then dipped nose-first back to the street below.

Polly suddenly saw something. "There!"

Below them, the primary Wing flew along, thinking it had escaped. Seeing his target, Sky Captain rocketed toward the machine just as the three pursuit Wings descended behind him. Sparks from enemy bullets danced along the Warhawk's fuselage. The leaky fuel line burst into flames again.

Sky Captain glanced back at the burning wing of his aircraft. "Yeah, right. A shortcut."

"I got us here, didn't I?"

12

An X on the Map
The Mysterious Woman Returns
A Watery End

Ducking from the crashing battle that continued in the skies above the Flying Legion base, Dex strained to listen to the chatter from Sky Captain's radio. He could hear the shouts, the chase, the gunfire in the background.

With charts strewn all over the table, he marked point after point on the world map as the signals came in. His oscilloscope displayed converging patterns. Dex unwrapped another wad of bubble gum and nervously popped it into his mouth, just to calm himself.

"Tell me you got something, Dex!" Sky Captain's ragged voice came over the loudspeaker. "We're getting clobbered up here."

Meanwhile, the attacking batlike Wings bombarded the base's power station, and a surge of electricity shot out from the oscilloscope's control panel. Sparks flew, but Dex shunted circuits, trying to get the signal back. Muffled explosions and high-caliber gunfire rattled the main hangar. Gaps of smoke-stained sky shone through holes in the corrugated roof.

"It's no picnic down here either, Cap," he shouted into the microphone. "Hang in there. We've almost got it."

*   *   *

Sky Captain and Polly continued down the one-way street after the primary Wing, desperate not to lose its tracking signal. The three pursuing Wings closed in behind the P-40, only a few plane lengths to the rear.

Unexpectedly, the primary Wing backflapped its metal wings and plunged toward the street, intentionally stalled in the air. Sky Captain's Warhawk swept past, narrowly missing it. "Awww, a kid pilot's trick and I fell for it!"

Its feint successful, the primary Wing gathered itself and climbed back up, shooting furiously at the Warhawk's tail. Now four of the attacking craft hammered away at Sky Captain.

"At least we don't have to worry about losing the primary Wing now," Polly said. "He's right on our tail."

Sky Captain yelled into his microphone. "Dex!"

"Thirty seconds, Cap. That's all I need."

"Thirty seconds?" How could the young man sound so calm?

"Plus or minus . . ."

Polly leaned over Sky Captain's shoulder and grabbed the microphone out of his hand. Bullets pinged into the plane, sparking off the rudder and the fuselage. She clicked the transmit button. "Dex hon?"

"Yeah, Polly?" Dex answered, his voice bright.

"Hurry!"

Sky Captain snatched the microphone from her hand. "I'm going to lead them out over the water to try and buy us some time." He turned back to Polly, who looked breathless and overwhelmed in the back of the cockpit. "I tried to warn you. Still glad you came?"

Sky Captain pulled back on his flight stick as he rocketed through Times Square. The Warhawk shook and groaned as it shot high into the clouds, away from the streets of Manhattan.

Still firing, the Flying Wings closed in.

At the Legion's besieged base, searchlights scanned the heavens while shells exploded all around. The entire landing field and most of the hangars were ablaze as more batlike machines descended. The Flying Legion could barely hold its own as their planes circled and charged, guns blazing, in a desperate dogfight over their own turf.

With all the chaos, Dex had a hard time concentrating on his charts as technicians shouted out coordinates. "Thirty degrees, bearing zero zero five!"

Dex continued to mark lines on the map with a compass, pressing the point into the paper, sketching careful arcs. With each new coordinate, he drew the circle closer and closer to the vital position of the controlling signal.

Suddenly, a soot-stained Legion officer raced in, glancing from side to side until his gaze settled on Dex. "We can't hold them off any longer. We have to evacuate the base."

Dex stood his ground even as the building began to collapse around him. With a groan, a large chunk of the roof bent inward, dangling by a few ragged strips of metal. "Not yet. I'm almost there."

"There's no time, Dex! We have to go *now*!"

"Go ahead without me. I'm right behind you, but I don't intend to let Cap down."

Some of the technicians fled, while two remained at their stations, shouting out one more coordinate and then another, until Dex had isolated a tiny spot on the map. He drew an X through mountainous, barely charted terrain. "Got you!" Then he shouted into his microphone, "Joe, I found him! Joe!"

Dex's grin was short-lived as a massive explosion

rocked the control room, a direct hit from one of the attacking Wings. He grabbed for the map, crinkling the paper in his fingers as he went flying. Everything spun, tumbled, crashed. He struck the cement floor hard, wincing as his ribs and shoulder absorbed the shock.

Shaking his head, Dex looked down to see that he still clutched a small piece of map he'd torn from the larger chart as he fell. At least it was the section with the X drawn on it.

As he listened to the roar of flames and collapsing debris all around him, Dex tried to move, but looked down to see that his leg was pinned under a pile of fallen concrete and steel. He pulled at his leg, but to no avail. Although the pain hadn't kicked in yet, he knew it would probably be a screamer. If only he'd finished building that antigravity generator . . .

With a deliberate scraping sound, something large and powerful tore a wider opening in the hangar wall. From outside, a smoky haze obscured details, but Dex could see the ominous shapes form as they strode closer. Unable to run, he propped himself up, staring.

The trim figure of a dark-robed woman wearing large opaque glasses stepped imperiously over the rubble. She looked around, her impenetrable lenses seeming to scan the hangar's smoky interior. Flanking her were two seven-foot-tall walking robots. Each had a bullet-shaped head, a wasp-thin waist, and a pair of steel tentacles for arms. The tentacle arms twitched and thrashed, throwing off sparks as they touched the fallen debris.

Though pinned under the collapsed wall, Dex searched the rubble for any way to defend himself. His eyes widened when he spied his new prototype ray gun lying only a few feet away. If the sonic atomizer could melt a hole through a thick plate of steel, he knew it would make short work of those mechanical men.

The mysterious woman saw him, then strode toward him.

Caught in the rubble, Dex strained to reach the ray gun, but his fingers only grazed it. Finally hooking a knuckle around one of the decorative fins, he drew the futuristic weapon closer. At last he scooped it into his hand, turned the emission nozzle toward the nearest of the two tentacled robots, and fired a volley of concentric shimmering energy rings.

The beam from the sonic atomizer slammed into the robot's midsection, and the metal armor of its torso glowed white-hot. Its tentacles flailed, throwing off wild sparks, and the walking robot slumped forward, dropping to the piles of rubble on the hangar floor, as dead as a machine could be.

"One down!" Dex turned to fire at the second walking robot, but it was too quick for him. Serpentine coils lashed out, wrapping around Dex's wrist, and a flash of pain made him drop the ray gun. Another steel-cable tentacle easily swept the heavy rubble aside, freeing Dex's leg. Then the robot wrapped a tentacle around his waist and lifted him into the air like a doll.

Dex struggled in vain, unable to wrest himself from the robot's grasp. The tentacles tightened. He looked at the torn map fragment in his hand, desperate. Wheels were turning in his head.

As he rocketed away from the city and out over the metal gray Atlantic, Sky Captain dodged another volley of machine gun fire. By now the flames from the damaged fuel line had gained strength, engulfing the plane's wing.

Swallowing hard, Polly looked out the back of the cockpit, then turned forward again. She scribbled furiously on her reporter's pad, mouthing the words out loud as she wrote them. "Six Flying Wings on . . .

our . . . tail. Escape seemed . . . impossible. Out-manned. Outgunned. Hopeless . . ."

"Do you always have to write out loud?" Sky Captain yelled. "It's already hard enough to think around here!" The Warhawk took another hit and shuddered violently. Any other airplane would have been sky wreckage long before this; however, even with its specially installed systems, the P-40 could not endure such a pounding. "I can't outrun them much longer."

The Flying Wings continued to bombard their victim, and fire blanketed the entire left wing. Black smoke poured from the exhaust manifold, causing the plane to sputter, choke, and stall. Below, there was no way to escape, no place to land except the deep ocean.

"Hold on! They'll never expect this." Sky Captain unexpectedly shoved down on his flight stick, sending the Warhawk straight toward the choppy Atlantic. With one engine stalled, he had very little control left.

"Joe! What are you doing?" Polly peered through the windshield to see the ocean coming fast at them. "We're heading straight down. You'll kill us."

"I know what I'm doing. Try to relax, would you?"

"We're going too fast. We're not going to make it. You have to pull up." Polly grabbed the shoulder of his leather jacket, but he did not flinch. "Pull up, Joe! *Pull up!*"

Sky Captain struggled with the controls as the Flying Wings regrouped. The Warhawk continued to accelerate downward, assisted by gravity. They hurtled toward the ocean's murky surface . . . sure to die.

episode 3

"SHADOW OF TOMORROW"

Dex has located the source of a mysterious radio transmission, but captured by Dr. Totenkopf's deadly machines, he is unable to warn Sky Captain.

Meanwhile, Sky Captain's Warhawk has been attacked by strange flying machines and is about to crash into the ocean's surface.

13

A Remarkable Capability
Underwater Ace
A Base in Flames

Only seconds from crashing into the water, the P-40's engine sputtered, then briefly roared back to life. Sensing the end of the chase, the Flying Wings zoomed after them.

Polly screamed. Sky Captain kept his stranglehold on the controls, never swerving. The ocean came at them like an endless expanse of blue pavement. Polly closed her eyes, bracing for the crash.

Moments before impact, Sky Captain shouted through his headset microphone, "Switching to amphibious mode!" His right hand slapped an emergency switch.

A series of servomechanisms clicked into place. Hull vents and exhaust manifolds sealed shut. Gaskets clamped around the cockpit canopy, and the engine droned at a lower octave. The Warhawk transformed into a sleeker bullet shape, like a flying torpedo.

Then Sky Captain's plane plunged into the choppy water.

The sounds became immediately muffled as the diving aircraft submerged in a froth of bubbles. The fire on the wing was instantly extinguished, and the propeller's growl became a more sonorous hum. The Warhawk jetted along underwater.

Above, the streaking enemy Wings collided with one another, some swerving, some slamming into the ocean. Broken chunks of hulls, wings, and engines splattered like a meteor storm into the Atlantic.

As the P-40 cruised along beneath the waves, going deeper, Polly kept her face pinned to the window, stunned. "We went . . . underwater!"

Sky Captain calmly piloted the plane along. "Yeah, Dex rigged it up. Got the idea from one of his comic books. Good old Dex."

Barely a month went by without Dex showing him some of his favorite literature, be it the colorful pages of a superhero comic or the black pen-and-ink drawings in *Amazing* or *Astounding*. The young man had invented sensors, supercharged engines, electrical armor (which shorted out more often than not), even new prototype weapons, like his "Buck Rogers" sonic atomizer.

Since the evil geniuses of the world continued to create innovative threats, Sky Captain and the Flying Legion had to develop new ways to counter them. Dex continued to read his science fiction voraciously, purely for research purposes.

Now, as Polly's terror melted away, angry realization crossed her face. "You knew this, and you let me think we were going to crash?" She shoved the back of his pilot's chair. "Damn it, Joe! I thought we were both going to die! You should have said something!"

"I was a little busy trying to save our lives. Besides, *you* wanted to come aboard, adding about a hundred and fifty pounds of extra weight and hampering my maneuverability."

"A hundred and *fifty*! Why you—"

"Just a guess."

"You still should have told me."

The currents streamed by, carrying a flow of white bubbles away from the churning propeller. Filtered sunlight provided barely enough illumination for Sky Captain to see by, though he didn't have a particular destination in mind. He sounded exasperated with her. "Look, Polly, if you can't take it, it's not my fault."

Though she seethed, Polly's natural toughness came through. "I can take it. I can take anything you dish out."

"Good because this was nothing. Just a practice run." He reengaged the main engines. Yanking on the stick, he guided the Warhawk up toward the bright sunlight.

As Sky Captain's plane burst through the surface, water sprayed, and the drone of the propeller changed again. He leveled the plane off and banked about, turning toward dry land. "Ready to head back to the base?"

In the distance, he could see pieces of the destroyed enemy Wings continue to rain down into the water. He couldn't help but look at the dissipating stain without feeling smug pride.

Sky Captain heaved a sigh and lifted the cockpit microphone. "Dex, come in. Please tell me you got what we needed." He paused, waited, then frowned. "Do you read me? Hello, Dex . . . ?"

But only the steady hiss of static came back at him. He and Polly exchanged a concerned glance; then he accelerated back toward land, setting course for the Flying Legion's base. On the way, he tried again and again to raise Dex or anyone. The Legion's private frequency remained ominously silent.

His stomach knotted as they flew overland, crossing the hilly wilderness, approaching the huge complex where his mercenary squad had established their headquarters. The pillars of smoke were visible long before he reached the sheltered valley.

When the base came into view at last, it seemed everything was in flames. As the scope of the destruction became apparent, Sky Captain could find no words to express his dismay.

Polly whispered hoarsely, "My God . . . Joe!"

The hangars were burning. Dozens of parked fighter aircraft, once neatly lined up and ready for takeoff, smoldered along the runway. The observation zeppelins lay slumped on the ground like blackened whale skeletons. Sky Captain could see many crashed enemy Wings, but he also spotted the wreckage of Legion aircraft that had been defending the base—far too many of them.

14

A Missing Friend
A Robot Infestation
A Secret Message

The hard part was finding a clear patch of pavement in the disaster zone. Emergency crews were everywhere, dousing flames and pulling victims from the rubble. Sharp wreckage from the explosions and crashes lay scattered all about.

Sky Captain was numb and sick as he circled for the second time, but he drove back his feelings and focused on the job at hand. He had to get down safely.

One tire on the P-40's landing gear hit a torn metal plate sticking out of the softened blacktop. The War-hawk slewed, but Sky Captain drove forward, his brakes smoking and screeching. The plane bounced over a shallow crater and finally came to a halt in front of what had been a secondary maintenance hangar.

Grease-stained, red-eyed crewmen stumbled toward his plane. They rejoiced to see Sky Captain alive, drawing strength and hope from their leader. The crackling sound of fires was a background roar in the air. The task of simply extinguishing all the fires and rescuing the wounded seemed insurmountable, but the members of the Flying Legion remained undaunted.

Sky Captain climbed from the cockpit and stood on

his bullet-riddled wing. Polly came out behind him, and he extended a hand to her, distracted by the chaos around him. She was too shocked to comment on his help.

Jumping to the ground and brushing himself off, Sky Captain turned toward the control hangar, where a group of men was straining to clear a heavy steel beam that blocked the doorway to the map room. They were trying to rig up a block and tackle, but could not find an intact support beam for the chain.

Seeing him, one of the crewmen called out urgently. "It's Dex, Cap! They've got *Dex*."

Sky Captain's distraught look transformed to rage as he took charge. "No time to mess with a chain and pulley. Unless you men can find one of Dex's disintegrator pistols, let's do this the old-fashioned way." Crouching, he leaned into the solid beam, using all his might to push. "We've got enough muscle around here. Help me."

Working together, the men pushed the steel girder aside with sheer brute force. The beam finally gave way with a sound of twisting metal, dropping to the ground with a heavy *clang*. Sky Captain stood up to catch his breath and saw that they had opened a narrow tunnel into the map room.

Polly squeezed through the small passageway beside Sky Captain to enter the ruined building. The two of them emerged in the map room, which had become a nightmarish scene.

Walking robots were everywhere. A dozen of the man-sized machines marched about with mechanical precision, whiplike steel tentacles thrashing from their shoulder sockets. The coiled arms picked up furniture and equipment, tossing wreckage aside. The robot walkers moved through the map room like insects, obviously searching for something.

"They're everywhere," Polly said. "It's an infestation."

One of the machines detected the intruders and strutted toward them. Sky Captain turned just as the walking robot lashed out with a surprisingly long tentacle. Polly shouted a warning, but the appendage wrapped itself around Sky Captain's right hand, drawing tight like a python. He reached awkwardly with his left hand to pull out his sidearm. The robot tightened its snakelike metal grip as he twisted his body, managed to aim the pistol, and fired off one round. The bullet found its target, shattering the robot's single gleaming optical sensor. The spindle-waisted machine recoiled, rocking backward like a jack-in-the-box. The tentacle released Sky Captain's wrist and flailed about. The robot staggered blindly before it fell in a heap.

The struggle alerted the rest of the robot swarm, and all of them turned their singular glowing eyes toward Polly and Sky Captain. Marching in an eerily gliding lockstep, the machines closed in from all sides. Polly stepped close as Sky Captain fired his pistol at another machine; the bullet smashed its blunt head, deactivating the robot in a shower of sparks. He knew how many rounds he had in the pistol and saw that there were far too many of the machines.

"We've got to be a lot more efficient at this," he said. The walking robots stepped closer, raising jointed steel legs to climb over the rubble.

Then Sky Captain looked up to the collapsed roof. Suspended directly above them, a massive girder dangled by the frayed remnants of two cables. The robots marched under its shadow.

Sky Captain stepped back to lure the machines closer. Then he raised his pistol, squinted carefully along the sight line, and fired. The bullet clipped the cable holding the heavy beam in place; the remaining line groaned as the released girder swung down like a giant pendulum.

He yanked Polly to the floor as the twisted beam

whistled over them, missing their heads by inches. The battering ram swung into the front row of machines and crushed them with a sound like a truck full of brass musical instruments ramming a brick wall.

Sky Captain and Polly sprang to their feet, ready to face the rest of the robot swarm, but before the walking machines could form ranks again, a strange alien siren warbled through the air.

"What's that, Joe? A Legion signal?"

"Not one of ours," he said.

The walking robots froze in their tracks, tentacle arms drifting like seaweed in a gentle current. Then, all the remaining machines scattered like cockroaches, escaping through the gaping hole in the hangar wall. One of the machines stumbled on a loose chunk of concrete and collided with a second robot as if it were part of a slapstick comedy routine, but both righted themselves and evacuated through the opening.

Sky Captain looked down at his sidearm. "That was easy."

"We can't just let them get away, Joe. They've got Dex."

Both of them scrambled over the rubble, chasing the walking robots. When they reached the hole in the wall, though, a backwash of exhaust fumes and air currents knocked them backward. Sky Captain kept his balance, squinting into the hot gust to see one of the large Flying Wings rise up. The enemy aircraft took off, stealing away with the remaining tentacled robots.

"Hey!" Sky Captain waved his pistol and fired repeatedly at the flying machine until all his ammunition was gone. The small-caliber bullets merely bounced off the quicksilver hull.

"They're getting away, Joe. We have to stop them!"

She looked wildly around, but Sky Captain stopped her. "It's too late. They're gone."

"They've got Dex, Joe. We have to try."

Polly resisted, but he continued to hold her. "They're gone," he said again, "for now."

She slowly accepted defeat. They stood together, watching in vain, as the last enemy ship arched skyward. Nightfall had darkened the sky, and the batlike Wing flapped upward to join a dozen of the enemy flying machines that converged overhead. Their angular silhouettes crossed the full moon, gaining altitude, remaining impossibly out of reach.

Sky Captain and Polly stood side by side, sighing and staring at the complete destruction of the Legion's headquarters. Orange flames still smoldered like the bonfires of a primitive army encampment. Some surviving crewmembers worked together to spray water on the blazes; others used flashlights and crowbars to search for wounded men in the collapsed storehouses.

"Of all the enemies we've faced, this is the worst blow the Flying Legion has ever suffered." Sky Captain couldn't even begin to assess the casualties and the irreparable damage.

With a loud screeching groan, the last wall of a destroyed shed collapsed.

Polly shook her head, staring across the blasted runways. "Why would Totenkopf do this, Joe? Why Dex? It doesn't make any sense."

"I don't know enough about him to make a guess. Usually villains are all too happy to brag about their capabilities and gloat over their plans." Sky Captain turned back to the remains of the map room, peering into the dimness. Dex had stayed at his post until the last minute, trying to triangulate the source of the command transmission for the robot giants and the Flying Wings.

Stepping back into the hollow-sounding room, he saw a stack of Dex's comic books and pulp magazines scattered across the stained floor. He spotted scuffed footprints, drag marks from robot feet, the signs of a struggle. With a grim frown, he bent over to pick up a torn comic book. A smear of drying blood tracked across the fanciful cover illustration. He pondered for a moment, then looked up at Polly. "Totenkopf was looking for something—something he thinks we have."

Sky Captain tossed the magazine to the floor and reached down to pick up the prototype ray gun. "Dex said he knew where the transmission was coming from, but I didn't give him enough time to answer me."

A flash of guilt crossed Polly's face. She knew she had withheld information from Sky Captain, especially the two mysterious vials. What if her secrecy had inadvertently led to Dex's capture? If Sky Captain had known all the details, might he have been better prepared?

Sky Captain continued to contemplate the Buck Rogers sonic atomizer, not looking at her. "He must have gotten too close to the answer. Dex was trying to tell me—"

Having second thoughts about her secrecy, Polly reached into her pocket and started to withdraw the two test tubes Dr. Jennings had given her as his last act. She looked at the glass vials. She knew Sky Captain would be furious with her for keeping secrets.

Before she could make up her mind to tell him, though, Polly spotted something on the floor among the clutter. She slipped the test tubes back into her coat and reached down to brush the rubble aside. A bubble gum wrapper, the brand Dex always chewed. "Joe . . ."

Sky Captain turned the ray gun over in his hand, then stuffed it into his pocket. Polly stared at him, holding up the gum wrapper as if it carried extra meaning. He followed her eyes, curious, as she glanced upward. A slow smile spread across her face.

On a fallen section of the ceiling, Sky Captain saw

a torn section of map stuck there, out of reach, with a pink wad of gum. The chart scrap showed pinpricks from a compass, several tentative markings that circled down to a bold X drawn in the center.

"Good boy, Dex!" Sky Captain let out a relieved laugh. His expression was different now.

"This changes everything," Polly said, sharing his delight.

"But it's still personal. We leave right away—while we have a chance. There's a long way to go."

The word *NEPAL* was printed plainly across the center of the map.

15

Off to Nepal
A Satchel Full of Secrets
The Mark of Unit Eleven

The Warhawk soared into the night, heading east across the Atlantic. After the robotic mayhem in recent days, Polly thought the long journey might almost seem relaxing. The droning sound of the engine would have made a good lullaby, if both she and Sky Captain hadn't been so tense.

The P-40 had been refueled, its machine guns reloaded, its burned fuel line repaired. Three of the Legion's best engineers and mechanics had given the plane a rushed inspection, patching up the worst bullet holes in the fuselage and pronouncing the craft ready to launch.

Without much celebration, the crewmen waved the Warhawk onto the base's only intact runway. "Go get them, Cap!"

Even in the best of times, a journey halfway around the world would have been arduous. They'd need to refuel in London and probably Istanbul or Samarkand before making a final run to the Himalayas. Thanks to their prior adventures, the Flying Legion had allies everywhere. Sky Captain didn't doubt that the Warhawk would perform admirably, as it always did.

They had to rescue Dex—and stop Totenkopf.

Once again, Polly sat in the back of the tight cockpit. It was going to be a long ride, but she wouldn't give Sky Captain the satisfaction of complaining. If he could put up with the arduous journey, so could she. Intent on the cockpit controls, he didn't seem to mind her silence. Polly could sense he wanted to talk to her, but she decided to let him make the next move. Maybe he wanted to apologize. . . .

In the cramped confines of the rear seat, lit only by glowing green cockpit gauges and indicators, Polly set Dr. Jennings's scuffed satchel on her lap. Until now she hadn't had a quiet moment to look through the documents inside. She scanned page after page of scientific notations, numbers, and graphs. She saw scrawled journal entries written in German and wished she had brought her translation dictionary with her. But it was at her desk in the *Chronicle* offices, along with her typewriter.

Nevertheless, she had her reporter's pad and could take copious notes. Her camera had plenty of film, extra rolls were in her pack. When she saw Editor Paley again, she would have a great story for him. . . .

The largest and most impressive documents in the satchel were blueprints of numerous strange machines. Many of the designs looked familiar to her—the tentacled robot walkers, the Flying Wings, the towering mechanical monsters that had invaded Manhattan. She saw other design sketches of ominous devices, all of which looked as if they had sprung from the wild nightmares of Leonardo da Vinci.

After making sure that the pilot couldn't see what she was doing, Polly shifted the satchel and reached into her coat pocket to withdraw the two mysterious test tubes. With his dying breath, Jennings had warned that these vials would be the end of the world if they fell into the hands of Dr. Totenkopf. She studied them, then scribbled a series of notes in the margin of her pad: *Virus? Explosive? Poison?* Finding no answers, only guesses, Polly carefully wrapped the test tubes in a piece of cloth and returned them to her pocket.

By now she was starting to find Sky Captain's stubborn silence oppressive. She rummaged loudly, rustling more papers in the satchel, and finally spoke. "It looks like these journals belonged to Dr. Jorge Vargas. He must have passed them on to Dr. Jennings before his disappearance."

"Vargas? Wasn't he the man who vanished right after the *Hindenburg III* docked?"

She brightened. "Why, Joe, you read my newspaper article."

"I heard it on the radio."

Polly didn't rise to the bait, pointedly looking back at the satchel's contents.

Sky Captain continued. "Vargas must have considered those papers important then. Jennings certainly did." He turned around to see her shaking her head in wonder. "What did you find?"

"Just some amazing background information." Polly lifted one of the typed dossier pages. "Totenkopf was awarded his first patent when he was only twelve years old." She flipped to another page and continued reading, deciphering the German as best she could. "By seventeen he had already received two doctorates and was one of the most highly regarded minds of his day. All of that was before the start of the Great War."

She paused. "Then a darker side began to emerge. First, animals started disappearing in his village—only to be found later, dead and mutilated, victims of unthinkable experiments. Then children . . ." Polly looked up, her expression sickened in the wan cockpit light. "Reports of missing children."

She found a loose folder inside the satchel and

opened it to reveal curling old photographs. "One year after Totenkopf's disappearance, ominous rumors began circulating in the German Parliament, whispers that he had begun work on what was darkly hinted to be a"—she struggled with the translation—"a doomsday device. For decades, all efforts to locate Totenkopf have consistently failed. To this day, his whereabouts remain a mystery."

"How long has it been?"

"No one has seen him for more than thirty years."

"Judging from all those robots striking cities around the world, he seems to have been busy in the meantime." He glimpsed Polly opening a ledger. "What's that?"

Polly answered in a monotone. "Nothing that makes any sense." She flipped back and forth, comparing pages. "These are Unit Eleven's supply logs. One section lists page after page of plant and animal life. Two of every species. Thousands of them." She rummaged in the satchel again, puzzled. "Stockpiles of enough food and supplies to last a decade. Reserves of steel, oil, coal."

"Quite the wish list."

Suddenly, Polly recognized what she was reading. She remembered what Dex and Sky Captain had told her in the warehouse of odd prototype robots. "This is everything he's used his machines to collect over the last three years, plus other items he still needs! And here at the bottom, the ledger even includes the power generators from Manhattan. It reads like a shopping list from all over the world." Polly's voice grew hushed with awe. "What have you been up to, Dr. Totenkopf?"

Though she continued to study the documents, she made no further connections, reached no remarkable conclusions. After a moment, she realized that Sky Captain had fallen into his sullen silence again. He stared intently out the window while dawn began to break over the British coast, as if he could make them arrive at their destination faster by the sheer force of his will.

A thoughtful look crossed Polly's face, and her heart went out to him. "He'll be okay, Joe. Dex can take care of himself."

Sky Captain slowly turned to look over his shoulder. He didn't seem to know what to say.

"We'll find him," Polly reassured him.

The Warhawk flew onward.

16

A Camp in the Himalayas
A Sherpa Friend
Destination: Shangri-La

Sky Captain's battered and reliable P-40 descended through a dense patch of cumulus, revealing the wrinkled and rugged contours of the earth, very close to the height of the clouds. High rocky peaks protruded from the cottony white ocean like jagged islands in an uncharted sea. Polly looked through the frost-etched cockpit canopy as the epic slopes of the Himalayas came into view.

"Those icy peaks are the Kanchenjunga Range," Sky Captain said like a tour guide. "We're crossing over the Tibetan Plateau."

"How close are we to Nepal?" She had tried not to ask the question too often during their lengthy flight, in which they had circled half of the globe.

"Right down there. If this were an atlas, you could see the letters on the ground." He took the Warhawk in a steep dive, plunging into the thick clouds. Polly didn't know how he could see the hazards, the treacherous peaks, the snowfields. But he flew on anyway, blind and confident.

Beneath the cloud layer, Sky Captain leveled them off, cruising along toward the base of the massive mountains. Polly saw windswept tundra, glaciers, naked boulders—and then a cluster of meager shelters and fur-lined tents spread out over a frozen lake bed.

"That's the base camp." He smiled. "All the comforts of home. We'll start there."

"We're a long way from Manhattan," Polly said.

As the P-40 circled overhead, a stout Nepalese Sherpa stepped out of a small shelter. He lifted his mittened hands to wave up at Sky Captain's plane.

"Ah, there's Kaji. He's expecting us." Two more men stepped out beside Kaji, gazing warily at the plane. All three were dressed alike in thick sheepskins, fur hats, and fleece-lined boots. The other two Sherpas did not wave.

The Warhawk glided to a smooth landing on the expansive white lake, kicking up crusty snow. Sky Captain taxied back along the icy surface until he rolled to a stop. Kaji and the other two Sherpas ran out onto the frozen lake to greet them as the pilot cut his engine.

When Sky Captain slid open the canopy, Polly gasped at the biting cold, but she bundled herself as well as she could. Sky Captain climbed out onto the plane's battle-scarred wing, then offered her a gloved hand. The lake's iron-hard ice was rough enough not to be slippery. As she stood there, Polly concentrated on not shivering.

Kaji came up to greet them, a ball of energy. He was in his late forties, but his weathered face had been etched by a lifetime of cold wind and blowing snow. "Captain Joe, my friend! I'm so glad to see you again."

"Good to see you, too, Kaji. I just wish it was under better circumstances." He gestured to Polly. "This is Polly Perkins. She's coming with us."

"How do you do?" she said, remembering her manners.

Kaji greeted her warmly, shaking her hand. "If Captain Joe has brought you along, then I am sure you can handle the rigors of the journey."

"She will," Sky Captain answered. It sounded like an ultimatum. He climbed back into the cockpit. "Let's get these supplies stowed."

Bellowing in Nepalese, Kaji spouted orders to his fellow Sherpas. One of them had a heavy brow, and the other sported a narrow hooked nose; both moved furtively, even in the open daylight. The two Sherpas took heavy boxes from Sky Captain as he unloaded them and set them on the wing. While Polly stood with her arms wrapped around herself to conserve warmth, the three Sherpas rapidly made an impressive pile of small crates and boxes.

"No wonder the cockpit was cramped," Polly muttered, looking at all the material.

Sky Captain handed a crate to the hook-nosed Sherpa as he spoke to Kaji. "Did you get the maps I needed? Detailed local surveys?"

"Yes, all of them drawn by native guides. Guaranteed accurate. They are inside the main tent." Kaji grinned, showing several missing teeth; then he hesitated in a long, coy pause. "Did you, perhaps, remember . . . something for me, Captain Joe?"

With a proudly satisfied expression, Sky Captain ducked down into the cockpit for the last time, searching under the main seat. He withdrew a trio of large, flat boxes. "Three cases, just like you asked."

Kaji took the boxes with a reverence reserved for holy relics. "A most incredible reward." The older Sherpa eagerly tore open the flap of the top box and reached inside. He pulled out a small round canister, grinning as he held it out for Polly to see. "Vienna sausages." He was misty-eyed. "By the gods, it has been so long!"

Balancing the three cases on his broad shoulder,

Kaji stumped off across the frozen lake toward the makeshift base camp. "Come, I will show you the maps. You will be impressed, I think."

Her teeth chattering in the high-altitude chill, Polly looked at the two reticent Sherpas standing at the pile of supplies. As Kaji waddled off, she gave Sky Captain a meaningful glance. "How well do you know that Sherpa?"

"Kaji? He's an old friend. Why?"

"Something about him . . . and these other two. Call it intuition. I don't trust him."

Sky Captain lifted a heavy duffel bag and carried it around the side of the plane. "That's funny. He said the same thing about you." He hefted the duffel, then tossed it to Polly. "Here, make yourself useful."

Polly caught the bag, but didn't have time to brace herself, so she stumbled backward. Out of the corner of her eye, she saw the surly-looking Sherpas standing beside the piled supplies. She was sure the two Himalayan men exchanged an ominous glance.

Inside the main tent, which was lit by a hanging kerosene lantern, Kaji, Sky Captain, and Polly sat around a small wooden table. The cold wind whistled outside, flapping the loose fabric of the shelter. Grains of snow stole through the poorly sealed entrance flap, but Polly had changed into warmer clothes and donned a pair of men's large gloves. A steaming teapot hung from a tripod over a small fire of dried yak dung. She was warm enough now to concentrate on the detailed hand-drawn map spread on top of the wooden table.

Sky Captain rested his elbow on the corner of the chart. "Dex tracked the signal to this valley here, north of Karakal." He produced the torn piece of map Dex had stuck to the hangar ceiling with bubble gum. Smoothing the map fragment, then rotating it, he lined it up with Kaji's chart. The scale was similar.

He pointed to the spot where Dex had triangulated the robots' command signal. "This is where the transmission originated."

But even on Kaji's detailed local maps, the area indicated showed no markings, no name. It was like a blank spot on an old nautical chart. Terra incognita. "Why is there no writing here? What is this?"

When the older Sherpa saw the X Dex had marked on the scrap, his face became troubled. He spoke the word with hushed reverence. *"Shambhala."*

Polly had never heard of the place, but she brightened. "Oh? You know it?"

"It is forbidden." Kaji turned away from the chart, obviously unsettled. "It is believed to be the source of the Kalacakra—Tibetan magic. Those who live there are said to have supernatural powers."

Polly looked at Sky Captain, and both of them knew the answer. If Dex had been taken to that place, they had no choice but to go. "Can you take us there?" Sky Captain asked.

Kaji grew quiet. He studied the map, considering the idea, then looked at the three cases of Vienna sausages. He let out a resigned sigh. "No one has ever ventured so far, Captain Joe. It will be dangerous."

"Naturally. And?"

"Shambhala is said to be protected by the priests of the Kalacakra Lamasery." The weathered Sherpa raked his rheumy eyes from Sky Captain to Polly, then to his Vienna sausages, as if weighing his obligations. "If they find us there, they will kill us."

"Why?" Sky Captain rolled his eyes. "What's so special about this place?"

"Shambhala is known by many names, my friends," Kaji said. "To the Hebrew it is called Eden. To the ancient Greek, it was Empurios. You, however, may know it as . . . Shangri-La."

The flap of the tent suddenly flew open with an icy gust of wind as one of the two sullen Sherpa helpers pushed his head inside. Ignoring the two guests, the heavy-browed Sherpa spoke in Nepalese directly to Kaji.

The old man gave a brisk, incomprehensible answer, then turned back to Sky Captain and Polly. "There is a storm coming, and the way will grow dangerous. If you still wish to go, we must depart now."

Neither of them knew what dangers might lie ahead, but Sky Captain turned to Polly. They stared down at the unmarked region on the map, thinking of Dex and Totenkopf, then answered in unison, "Let's go."

17

A Treacherous Route
A Blank on the Map
A Frozen Base

At first the snowfall was deceptively light, though it thickened as the wind picked up and the clouds clustered more tightly around the peaks of the Kanchenjunga Range. Sky Captain, Polly, Kaji, and the other two Sherpas started up the mountain in a slow-moving caravan, dressed in warm clothes and carrying supply-laden backpacks. Clumped snow and slippery rocks made each step treacherous. The temperature seemed to drop every minute.

"Is there really supposed to be a trail here?" Polly asked, her head bowed into the wind.

"Not a trail," Kaji said. "It is a *route*."

"Not many people build blacktop roads into a forbidden land," Sky Captain pointed out, drawing a long breath of the thin, icy air. "Not even Dr. Totenkopf."

Kaji plodded ahead in his fleece-lined boots, not complaining. Behind them, the sinister pair of Sherpas followed, muttering to each other in Nepalese over the howling wind.

During the course of the day, as the storm settled over them and gave the party no respite, the climbers accomplished what seemed to be a humanly impossible journey. First they walked and then they climbed against the white vastness of the isolated mountain range. Taking it upon himself to watch out for Polly, Sky Captain had to save her life only three or four times: dodging avalanches, rescuing her from collapsing ice bridges, catching her gloved hand as she slipped off a precipice. He decided he would have been embarrassed if she'd showered him with too much gratitude.

As the snow piled up like frozen quicksand, the air grew more and more rare in the cliffs high above the base camp. Like solid workhorses, the three Sherpas did not slow despite the treacherous terrain, but Sky Captain and Polly found their feet dragging as they slogged along. A flurry of wind and sleet blanketed the party. He could barely see Kaji's white-crusted back and shoulders directly in front of him.

Halfway up the mountainside, the weathered Sherpa led the procession around a narrow ledge overlooking a deep ravine. Polly clung against the rough icy sides and glanced apprehensively into the abyss below. The yawning fissure seemed to split the Himalayas from India to Tibet. One misstep and she had no idea in which country her battered and frozen body would come to rest.

As if the very thought made the path more dangerous, brittle rock gave way under her foot, and Polly slipped. She windmilled her arms as a gust of wind pushed her over the edge, but Sky Captain's quickness saved her. He grabbed her by the arm and pulled her to safety. "That's five times today," he quipped.

"Four. Don't exaggerate."

Behind them, watching Polly's near fall, the two suspicious Sherpas moved up behind Sky Captain, seeing their chance. The hook-nosed one gave a silent but meaningful nod to his companion as he began to draw a curved dagger from within the warm folds of his sheepskin covering. The heavy-browed Sherpa, though, made a gesture that stayed his hand. In Nepalese, he quickly said, "Be patient." Both men knew there would be plenty of opportunities along the dangerous path to Shangri-La.

When the members of the party finally pulled themselves to the top of a narrow, exposed ridge, the mountain wind jabbed at them like swords. Polly and Sky Captain had to hold on to each other just to keep their balance.

The snow cleared, and scudding storm clouds moved about below, giving the travelers a bright view of icy peaks that stood high and remote in the distance. The two Sherpas pushed ahead, not wanting to rest next to their three companions. With a frown, Polly watched them go.

Sky Captain sidled up next to Kaji, who gazed into the sprawling Himalayan wilderness, undaunted by the frigid temperature. Extending a mittened hand, the Sherpa pointed toward the craggy peaks. "This is where civilization stops, Captain Joe. Ahead of us is only a blank on the map." He tightened his hat and his mittens. "We must be very careful from here."

Polly looked at Kaji, shivering. "I thought we needed to be careful back there, too."

"For all the good it did," Sky Captain said.

From the distant outcropping where they had stopped, the two other Sherpas began to shout excitedly. Kaji cocked his ears, listening to the Nepalese words, and then motioned for Sky Captain to follow him. "Come! Hurry!"

Summoning her last shreds of energy, Polly hurried after their guide as he climbed effortlessly up the final few feet of the mountain peak. The higher vantage let them see beyond the intervening ridge.

The last thing she expected to see was the impossibly huge shape of a transmitting tower rising from the deep mountain valley. The steel structure protruded above the tallest of the nearby crags, but its lower half was buried in snow.

Sky Captain stared, knowing the only person who could have built such a facility. "Totenkopf."

Polly came up next to him, panting. "From here at the top of the world, he could send commands to his robots anywhere!"

"He probably did. This is where Dex traced the signal."

When the wind died briefly, they could hear a low, electrical hum emanating from the gargantuan tower. A dim light blinked intermittently at its peak, though Sky Captain knew no aircraft would attempt to fly over the dangerous Kanchenjunga Range. He pushed ahead with renewed enthusiasm, scrambling down the steep and rocky path. "Come on. We're close now."

"Maybe they'll have hot coffee down there," Polly muttered to herself as she started after him.

"Tea, perhaps, but I do not think so," Kaji said.

When they reached the base of the massive tower, they stood knee-deep in snow. Sky Captain stopped in astonishment as the extent of the madman's Himalayan base became apparent. The high transmitting tower was merely the tip of Totenkopf's operations.

The transmitting structure was utterly dwarfed by the staggering vastness of an expansive subterranean excavation spreading out ahead of them. Immense blocky power stations stood like geometrical sentinels on either side of a gaping shaft entrance large enough for several of Sky Captain's Warhawks to fly inside. Transformers, ringed conical boosters, and thrumming storage banks created a technological storage dump around the barren rock. Spearlike icicles dripped from the exposed metal.

Sky Captain withdrew a pair of binoculars from his backpack and scanned the area, squinting against the bright snow. He could make out a shimmering maze of ice tunnels bored deep into a glacial mass and reinforced with steel beams. Other shafts in the mountain rock led to dark side chambers. Abandoned ore cars sat waiting on rails.

"What is it?" Polly looked on in awe, anxious to use the binoculars for herself. "Let me see."

But Sky Captain would not relinquish them. "It looks like a mining outpost." From the weathered appearance of the generators caked with ice and snow, the frozen ore cars, the drifts piling up on the fringes of the main shaft, he guessed that the mine had long since been uninhabited. Brute-force machinery had been left uncovered and unmaintained, ravaged by the effects of time.

Squinting, Kaji put his hands on his broad hips and stared at the distant forbidding sight. "Something bad happened here."

With his binoculars, Sky Captain followed the steel shape of a rail bridge that led into the mouth of the fantastic mine. Even with the mountain breezes, an eerie stillness cloaked the base. "It looks abandoned." He turned to Kaji. "Tell your men we're heading down there. I want to get a closer look."

Kaji nodded nervously. "Yes, Captain Joe. But this is . . . not a good place."

"It certainly isn't how I pictured Shangri-La," Polly said.

The older Sherpa turned to her. "No, not Shangri-La. Not here."

When they reached the huge generators that flanked the entrance to the gaping mine shaft, the five companions moved slowly inside the massive cave. The chilling moan of arctic winds echoed off the gorge walls behind them.

"At least inside here, we're sheltered," Sky Captain said.

"It's still not my idea of *cozy*," Polly said.

Wide-eyed, she stepped deeper into the fantastic cave. Suspended high above her, enormous stalactites of ice dangled from iron girders that crisscrossed the labyrinth. Giant drilling machines, heavy excavators, rail tracks, and ore cars cluttered the main chamber, all of them motionless.

Polly was the first to spot the emblem of a grinning iron-winged skull on all the equipment. "It's Totenkopf, all right."

Amid the clutter, Kaji found several old lanterns, which he managed to light. He handed one to Polly and another to Sky Captain, who led the way, driven by his own curiosity. "Dex!" he called once. The echoes shattering the frozen silence made him cringe.

As they walked slowly through the massive ice cave, reflected lights splashed against rugged glacial walls. Polly could see only dark shadows of strange shapes embedded deep within the thick ice—prehistoric creatures, fossilized remains from the last ice age, unearthed by Totenkopf's mining operation.

Accompanying them, Kaji seemed uninterested in the surreal exhibit. He wrinkled his wide nose. "The air smells like death, Captain Joe."

The five members of the group began to fan out, exploring. Polly walked along the base of one of the enormous but silent drilling machines. She wiped off a thick layer of sediment and dust. "Where is everyone?" The sound of her own voice spooked her.

Trying to hold her hands steady in the oppressive cold, she lifted her camera to snap a photo of the gargantuan machine. Before she clicked the picture, though, Polly noticed that the hook-nosed Sherpa had moved away from the others. Thinking he was unobserved, the man disappeared furtively down a dim side tunnel. . . .

*　　*　　*

Sky Captain and Kaji found an elaborate control panel set against a bank of diagnostic machinery on a far wall. They passed an abandoned screen that served as a communication terminal. All the lights were dark on the controls, though. Sky Captain flicked a few switches, but got no response. Looking down at a shelf behind the workstation, the Captain discovered a bound log.

"Maybe Totenkopf did some things the old-fashioned way." Removing his gloves, he opened the book and began flipping through the brittle pages covered with handwriting. "Curious. The last entry was made . . . twenty-five years ago."

The Sherpa poked among a row of glass specimen jars that contained ore samples. He lifted one of the dusty jars, rattled it, and pressed his face close to the glass to study the contents. "Rocks. What was your enemy looking for?"

Troubled by what he read, Sky Captain closed the old logbook in alarm. "Uranium. A very rich and pure vein." Then he saw Kaji holding the specimen jar. "I wouldn't touch that."

The Sherpa's eyes widened as he looked at the jar in his hand, then quickly set it back on the shelf with all the others. He wiped his hand on his sheepskin jacket.

Sky Captain turned from the log and the communications screen and found an equipment locker beside him. Rattling the latch, he forced the old handle on the locker, and the door creaked open. Inside, he found bulky white suits with glass helmets. "Radiation suits. It seems Totenkopf didn't take any chances."

On a shelf above the thick suits, Sky Captain found a small boxy device with a gauge on its face. Lifting the device by the handle on its top, he flipped a switch, then watched the needle on the gauge immediately swing over into the ominously marked red zone. A familiar raspy crackle emanated from a tiny speaker.

Kaji turned apprehensively toward him. "What is it, Captain Joe? What's that noise?"

"This is a Geiger counter." Sky Captain swung the device, pointing the detector end in another direction, but the speaker only squawked louder, becoming a staticky roar. "And that noise indicates radiation. A lot of it. This whole mine is contaminated." He continued to scan the room, but the Geiger counter found no place that wasn't saturated. "We can't stay here."

Concerned, he looked up, suddenly noticing that the others were missing. He couldn't see or hear any of them. He turned to Kaji. "Where's Polly?"

18

A Shadow in the Tunnel
Lies and Exaggerations
A Lit Fuse

Sensing that the hook-nosed Sherpa's mysterious behavior would lead to some answers—or at least to an interesting news story—Polly crept along the twisting passageway.

Though Kaji's two companions had pretended to be surprised at the discovery of Totenkopf's frozen mining complex, this man knew exactly where he was going and what he was doing. Forgetting the chill in the air, she moved tentatively forward, holding the sputtering kerosene lantern to light her way. Confident in his furtiveness, the sinister Sherpa did not notice her sneaking after him.

As she followed the hook-nosed Sherpa's shadow, Polly rounded a bend in the tunnel. Up ahead, the corridor widened into a dead-end chamber blocked by a great metal door with a wheel lock in its center. Surrounded by iron reinforcement strips and heavy rivets, the barricade looked like the hatch to an enormous German U-Boat. Her lamplight spilled across a warning sign hung over the hatch: *VERBOTEN*.

"I don't suppose this is the lunch-break room." Then she frowned, realizing that she could no longer see the furtive Sherpa, though he had nowhere to go except inside.

Curious, Polly stepped up to the heavy steel door, set her lantern on the stone floor, and used both hands to tug the locking wheel. Despite the abandoned appearance of the Himalayan facility, the mechanism was well oiled and maintained. The metal hatch swung wide.

After adjusting her backpack, she retrieved her lantern and held it in front of her as she entered the chamber. The rock-walled room was too large for the weak pool of light to do much good. Polly worked her way slowly into the pitch-black room, sweeping her lantern across the tunnel walls. She tried to be as quiet as she could. The place seemed cavernous, a huge storeroom of some sort. What had Totenkopf been doing in here? She saw stacked crates, wooden barrels—

Suddenly, her circle of lantern light fell upon the evil, grinning face of the hook-nosed Sherpa. He stood only inches from her, waiting with an outstretched knife. He pounced.

Polly reeled backward and let out a scream.

Sky Captain and Kaji moved cautiously down the tunnel. "Miss Perkins!" the Sherpa called.

"Polly!" Sky Captain's voice held more annoyance than concern. She was always wandering off, getting herself—or him—into trouble, or just losing her way. Back there in plain sight, the complex's main chamber was filled with giant drilling machines, deactivated robots, radioactive specimens, and a log full of information about Totenkopf's purpose here.

How much more did she want? Wasn't that enough to keep her interested?

The two men came to a fork in the tunnel, which led off in two divergent paths. He sighed. "Looks like

The *Hindenburg III* docks at the Empire State Building
after its maiden voyage.

Polly and Sky Captain, embarking on a mission to
save the world.

Joseph Sullivan, Sky Captain of the Flying Legion.

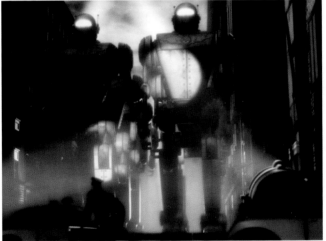

The evil Totenkopf's machines assault New York.

Flying robots swarm past the Flatiron Building.

Sky Captain takes to the heavens to defend New York City
in his P-40 Warhawk.

The battle against the machines rages on.

Polly and Joe encounter trouble on the way to find
Captain Franky Cook.

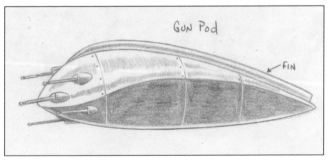

Production design sketch of the gun pod of a flying robot.

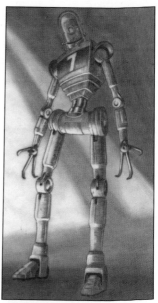

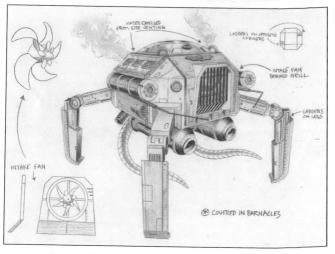

WATER EXPELLED
FROM SIDE VENTING

LADDERS ON OPPOSITE
CORNERS

INTAKE FAN
BEHIND GRILL

LADDERS
ON LEGS

INTAKE FAN

✗ COVERED IN BARNACLES

Design sketches of monstrous robots from the
film's preproduction.

Aircraft designs and a storyboard sketch from the film's preproduction.

we'll have to split up, Kaji. I'll meet you back outside, whether or not we find Polly. With the background radiation, don't stay here any longer than you have to."

Kaji nodded nervously. "Did you bring a Geiger counter, Captain Joe?"

"We don't need one anymore. Just assume the radiation is bad. Everywhere."

They each turned and proceeded down a different tunnel, calling out for Polly. Sky Captain strode along, grumbling, when he heard a woman's shrill scream coming from straight ahead of him. "Polly!" He raced down the tunnel, nearly slipping on the ice. His bobbing lantern threw weird patterns of light and shadow on the rough walls.

A moment later, he skidded to a stop at the storage chamber's open metal hatch. From inside Polly cried out again, a scream more angry than terrified, and he heard the sounds of a scuffle.

Sky Captain plunged into the room, waved his lantern around, and saw the Sherpa holding a knife to Polly's throat. She squirmed against the man's grip, but he pressed the blade against her soft flesh.

"Joe!" she cried.

Squaring his shoulders, Sky Captain stepped menacingly forward. A low growl came from his throat. "Let her go." He was ready to take the man apart with his bare hands.

Then, behind him, the heavy-browed Sherpa emerged from the shadows. He gripped a long curved knife of his own, poised to strike. "Give me the vials, and the girl will live." The man's intense eyes glittered in the lamplight.

"Vials?" Sky Captain's angry expression dissolved into one of confusion. "What vials?" He glanced a question at Polly, then turned back to the Sherpa with the heavy brow. "What are you talking about?"

"Do not play me for a fool, Sky Captain. I will not ask a second time." He nodded to his hook-nosed companion, whose thin lips twitched in a smile as he pressed the blade harder against Polly's skin and she squeaked.

Exasperated, Sky Captain put his gloved hands on his hips. "Look, I told you, I don't know what you're talking about." He lifted his chin. "You'll just have to kill us."

The Sherpa with the heavy brow shrugged. "As you wish. We can always search your corpses afterward." He nodded again, and his hook-nosed companion prepared to slit Polly's throat.

"Wait!" All eyes turned to Polly. The two Sherpas looked eager and hungry; Sky Captain, suspecting what she was up to, glared at her in exasperation.

Shrugging to loosen the hook-nosed Sherpa's suspicious grip, Polly worked her hand into her backpack, dug through the spare rolls of film, packets of food, and extra mittens, and hesitantly withdrew a small bundle of cloth she had tucked at the bottom. The dying words of Dr. Jennings ran through her head. If Totenkopf got his hands on these vials, it would be the end of the world.

But at the moment she didn't have a choice. Sooner or later, Sky Captain would figure out something . . . or she would have to do it for him.

Polly carefully unrolled the cloth to reveal the pair of sealed test tubes. The two Sherpas looked down, and their faces lit with evil expressions. She swallowed hard—at least the sharp knife was no longer cutting into her throat—and guiltily averted her gaze from the silent questions in Sky Captain's eyes. "I'm sorry, Joe."

The Sherpa with the hook nose snatched the tubes from Polly's hand. "This is most excellent. Now we have what we came for." Holding their knives ready, the two Sherpas slowly backed out of the room. "Good-bye, my friends. Your journey ends here."

The iron door swung closed behind them with a groan and a clang. By the light thrown off from the lanterns, they watched as the wheel lock clicked and spun shut. It was followed by the sound of a massive bolt sliding into place, like a gunshot echoing in the chamber. They were locked in.

Sky Captain turned to Polly, glaring. "Now . . . about those vials?"

She avoided him, more intimidated by his anger than she had been by the evil Sherpas. "I was going to tell you, Joe. You have to believe me."

"What was in them? Why are they so important?"

"I don't know. Really, I don't—"

He could not mask his contempt. "More lies." Frustrated, he paced over to the sealed metal hatch, yanked on the locking wheel, then kicked ineffectively against the door. Even with his thick boot, he hurt his toes.

"I'm telling the truth, Joe," she said, following him. "Dr. Jennings gave them to me just before he died. I don't know any of the details, but he said the countdown would begin and the world would end if Totenkopf got his hands on them. They were the last words he spoke."

Sky Captain found all this too incredible for words. "You expect me to believe that? You've done nothing but lie to me from the beginning." He kicked the door with his heel this time.

"Okay, I'm a liar, Joe, but I don't exaggerate. That's what Jennings said, back in his lab." Polly sniffed. "Wouldn't you tell the truth with your dying breath?"

"Unfortunately, you just might have a chance to find out." After straining against the locking wheel again, Sky Captain withdrew from the door. Then a realization formed in his mind. "So that's what Totenkopf was looking for all along: two test tubes. And he thought *we* had them? That's why he took Dex, and you didn't even tell me?"

"I'm sorry, Joe. I never meant for any of this to happen."

Fuming, he did not know what to say. Exhausted after all he had been through in the past couple of days, he squatted on the floor and leaned against the wall. Every step just got worse and worse. "Oh, did I tell you about the radiation? We've got to get out of here."

"No kidding."

With a frown, he turned away from Polly, listening intently. "Shhh." A faint hissing sound whispered through the air of the sealed room. "Do you hear that?"

For the first time since he had charged into the chamber, Sky Captain took the time to look around them. Standing again, he picked up one of the kerosene lanterns and held it high. "Where are we anyway?"

"I didn't have time to do much exploring, Joe. I had a knife to my throat."

Hundreds of wooden crates, reinforced barrels, and riveted metal boxes were stacked to the ceiling of the cavernous room. He stepped toward one of the crates, and Polly helped him pry open the lid. With a gloved hand, Sky Captain pushed packing straw aside to reveal neatly layered sticks of dynamite packed like sardines in a can.

His eyes slowly panned the room with a look of dread at the sight of the hundreds of containers that surrounded them. Now he read the bold stenciled German words: *SPRENGMITTEL* and *GEFAHR: DYNAMIT*.

"Does that say what I think it does?"

Polly nodded. "This room is full of explosives."

"Well, that's a little more immediate than background radiation." He let out another weary sigh. One of these days, he was going to have a lucky break.

All around them, the hissing sound grew louder. The two of them scanned the large chamber. At the same time, they both saw a dozen lit fuses lining the wall, out of reach. Sparks rapidly climbed the strands and moved across the high ceiling toward the crates of explosives that filled the room.

episode 4

"THE FLYING FORTRESS"

Sky Captain and Polly have tracked the mysterious radio signal to the treacherous mountains of Nepal. . . .

Trapped inside an ice cave filled with dynamite, Polly and Sky Captain have only seconds before the cave explodes.

19

A Final Confession
Outrunning a Fireball
A Reward for Treachery

Even if they climbed the stacks of crates and barrels, and if Polly stood on his shoulders, Sky Captain knew they could never reach the fuses—certainly not in time. The crackling trail of flame raced along, eating up the fuse, sizzling toward the stored dynamite. Totenkopf had enough explosives here to blast away half the mountain . . . as they were sure to find out in a few minutes.

Sky Captain and Polly ran to the thick metal door, hammering on it with their fists. "Kaji!"

Among the equipment piled next to the gunpowder barrels, Sky Captain spotted a rusty pickax with a weathered handle. He grabbed it, hefting the tool in a heavy arc. "Move!"

Polly ducked, and the pickax came down to strike the door with a bone-reverberating *clang*. Sky Captain shook his head to clear the ringing in his skull, then raised the tool and drove it down again and again. The sharp blade scored only a few shallow scratches on the armored hatch, nothing that qualified as so much as a dent. The tip of the rusty pickax bent upward, useless.

In disgust, Sky Captain dropped the pickax and knelt to feel along the sides of the hatch, probing for some gap in the frame. He couldn't pry with his fingertips, but maybe he could cram his own knife into a crack and use it like a crowbar. Nothing. Frustrated, he pounded his fist against the metal.

Polly lifted the lantern, swinging it around so she could search the walls, the floor, the ceiling. She hoped to find a ventilation shaft, a trapdoor, any means of escape, but quickly came to the realization that it was futile. "Joe? Just tell me something."

Sky Captain spotted a stray stick of dynamite lying at the base of the gunpowder barrels. He ran over to grab it. Overhead, the fuses continued their inexorable burning.

"In Nanjing"—she swallowed, not sure she wanted to know the answer—"You were running around on me with someone, weren't you?"

"No, Polly." Sky Captain's voice was firm, though his attention was focused on the loose stick of dynamite and the knife he drew from his belt. "And this isn't really the time to talk about hurt feelings."

Polly smiled, relieved. She seemed to forget about their danger. She would have given him a hug, but he was hammering and chipping at the floor with the blade tip.

Sky Captain succeeded in boring a small hole into the ice near the doorjamb. "There, that should be deep enough." He wedged and twisted the dynamite into place, then thought better of using the whole stick. He broke the dynamite in half and screwed the partial stick into the hole again. Then he used his knife to shorten the fuse. He stepped back, pushed Polly behind him, and withdrew his trusty lighter.

Coming out of her reverie, Polly saw what he meant to do. "Wait! What are you doing? As if there aren't enough—"

With the small blue flame from the lighter, Sky Captain ignited the stubby fuse. "I'll explain later. We've got only a few seconds right now." He grabbed her, and the two of them dove for cover behind a stack of wooden crates.

Polly saw that they had taken shelter behind more boxes of dynamite. "Oh good, we're safe."

Against his better judgment, he put his arm around her, and a calm came over both of them. Unspoken words stuck in his throat, and at last he blurted, "Polly, listen, this may be our last moment together. Remember what you said about telling the truth with your final words? There's something I need to know."

Polly leaned in closer, glad to be close to him. Like a nest of snakes, the fuses sputtered and burned closer to the tremendous detonation. "Yes?"

"Did you . . . did you cut my fuel line?"

Polly's face turned to rage. "Goddamn it, Joe! Why would you worry about something stupid at a time like this? I didn't sabotage your lousy airplane!"

"Fine." He still didn't sound as if he believed her.

"Our last moments in life, and this is all you have to say to me?" Polly shrugged away from him, suddenly seeming as cold as any glacier in the Himalayas.

He heaved a huge sigh. "Could we just for once die without all the bickering?"

Peeping around opposite sides of the piled crates, they watched as the fuse in the dynamite stick in the doorway burned down. Less than an inch remained. Despite themselves, Polly and Sky Captain looked at each other, then reluctantly drew together again to huddle for comfort.

"I'm not sure this is going to work," he said. "But at least it's a plan."

"At least it's a plan."

They were resigned to their imminent death as the fuses burned down. When all seemed lost, they both heard a sound at the thick metal door. The locking wheel rotated with a rapid series of clicks, and the heavy hatch swung open.

Kaji stood in the doorway, holding his lamp and grinning at them. "Ah, there you are, Captain Joe. And Miss Perkins. I have looked everywhere for you." He leaned inside. "Why have you locked this door?"

Its fuse almost completely burned, the half stick of dynamite dislodged and rolled at his booted feet. The Sherpa looked down at the explosive, then at the other sparkling fuses, the boxes of dynamite everywhere. "Oh, my!"

Bounding to their feet and racing for their lives, Polly and Sky Captain almost knocked Kaji over as they exited. "Run!" Sky Captain grabbed the other man, and the three scrambled down the tunnel.

Polly suddenly lurched to a stop and spun around. "Wait, my film! It's in the backpack!" She started back toward the chamber. Her pack lay against one of the dynamite crates.

Sky Captain grabbed her by the arm and roughly pulled her back as if he were reeling in a fish. "Leave it! There's no time." He shoved her in front of him as all three of them sprinted toward the wide exit. They passed the drilling machines, the shadowy frozen prehistoric forms, the communication screens, and the uranium samples. Sky Captain had never run so fast in his entire life, and he was pleased to see Polly and Kaji keeping pace. Blue sky and cold air lay just in front of them.

Inside the chamber, the first of the fuses finally reached the crates of explosives. It sputtered, fell silent for a brief moment, then erupted, the explosion igniting all the boxes nearby. Within fractions of a second, the flame front consumed and detonated the barrels of gunpowder. The chain reaction magnified the blast. The mine shaft did not merely explode; the ice and stone walls actually vaporized. Rock structures and ceilings collapsed. The mammoth mountainside began to sag under its own unsupported weight.

A tremendous ball of fire rushed down the tunnels, incinerating everything in its path. Like a stampeding beast, the blast shot down the shaft, devouring walls, steel rails, and tilted ore cars.

Sky Captain, Polly, and Kaji found themselves flung through the air by the outbound shockwave. As if they had been shot from a cannon, they flew until they dropped side by side into a deep snowdrift. Half buried in snow, the three companions ducked as a great wall of flame passed overhead.

Roaring echoes from the explosion ricocheted around the Himalayan crags, triggering distant avalanches that tumbled into deep, uninhabited gorges far below. The long shadows of twilight began to blanket the barricaded mountain valley.

Sky Captain could barely see in the dimness . . . or maybe his eyes or his head had been damaged. He sat up in the cold snow, his ears ringing. Was he half blinded? The angry rumbles continued as smoke and fire gushed into the thin air, and the worst noise subsided.

With a gloved hand, he wiped a smear of blood and soot from his face, trying to orient himself again. Beside him, he saw a woman's shape sprawled on the drift, not moving. He feared the worst. "Polly!" His voice sounded strange and distant in his own ears.

Dizzy, feeling the pulse pound inside his skull, he squinted into the white haze. The daylight seemed to be fading fast. He kept blinking.

A faint glow of flickering torches came out of the murk, bobbing flames carried in a winding procession. As his vision grew even fuzzier, Sky Captain saw a line of strange-looking natives approaching from the windswept horizon. They were dressed in thick black garments embroidered with odd symbols. Sagging hoods concealed their faces. He thought it might be a hallucination brought about by hitting his head.

As he began to pass out, Sky Captain reached weakly toward where Polly lay. He croaked out her name, but his voice was barely audible. He struggled in the soft snow, trying to move closer, but he finally dropped into unconsciousness. . . .

Holding up their torches, the natives gathered around the prone forms of Sky Captain, Polly, and Kaji. Without a word, they lifted the three figures, placed them on makeshift stretchers, then hoisted them up. Turning about in a smooth movement, the procession marched away into the frozen wilderness.

On a perch overlooking the devastated mine, the mysterious woman stood hidden from view. Turning her opaque goggles toward the fading smoke and flames, she observed the group of black-robed strangers take their captives and march away into the isolated mountain fastness.

They no longer concerned her.

She looked down to her black-gloved hand, where she held the pair of stolen test tubes. She clinched them in her fist, then turned back to the Flying Wing that rested precariously on a mountain ledge. It was time to go.

Without a downward glance, she stepped over the sprawled bodies of the two treacherous Sherpas, who lay facedown in a bloody patch of snow. Daggers had been driven through the men's backs with such force that they pierced their hearts and protruded from their chests. Soon, the frigid elements would destroy their bodies or scavengers would pick their bones clean.

The mysterious woman boarded the Flying Wing, activated the whistling engines, and glided away, leaving the Himalayas behind.

20

A Strange Procession
An Awkward Awakening
A Priest in Shangri-La

Night set in on the cold mountain passes. Hidden valleys lay surrounded by imposing rock walls and impenetrable cornices of snow, gendarmes of stone.

Though the black-robed natives carried torches, they did not need guidance. They picked their way down the winding slopes, carrying stretchers that bore Sky Captain, Polly, and Kaji.

The silent natives followed a secret, instinctive path. As they neared the crest of a saddle, crossing through a keyhole notch of sharply angled stone, the hooded leader paused to stare down into the newly revealed valley. Dense and frosty mists formed a veritable smoke screen, but the swirling shroud began to clear, revealing an image not unlike a desert mirage.

A surprisingly lush valley lay in the hazy distance. Sheltered on all sides by forbidding peaks, the secret valley was a feast of strange and heavenly beauty filled with flowing streams and orchards, stone monasteries and small huts adorned with colorful pennants. Beribboned prayer wheels on poles clacked in the breezes.

"Shangri-La," the hooded leader muttered, as he always did when he returned to his secret home. The black-robed natives moved forward. Incredibly, as they entered the valley, the wind and snow did not follow them.

Groaning on his stretcher, Sky Captain strained to open his eyes, trying to focus. He felt suddenly warm, calm, rested. He propped himself on one elbow and glanced behind him to the rear of the torch-carrying procession. Only a few feet away, a howling blizzard raged, but here the air was completely calm.

In front of him lay a tranquil valley, mysterious and inviting. He strained, mumbling. "Shangri-La . . ." But then he fell into a deeper, more restful sleep.

Golden sunlight bathed Polly's sleeping face in a warm glow. As she began to stir, languid and entirely at peace, she looked contented and beautiful. A smile inspired by gentle dreams curled her lips. She made a quiet, purring sound in her throat and snuggled deeper into the embroidered coverlet. With a sigh, she slowly fluttered her eyes open.

Disoriented but not troubled, she stared at a ceiling made of interlocking tiles, colored with hypnotic designs unlike anything she had ever seen before. After a moment, an odd expression came over her face like the shadow of a thundercloud. She shifted her body underneath the coverings again, and she lifted the embroidered blanket to peek beneath them. Suddenly, her eyes grew large and she yanked the blanket tight against her body.

"My clothes . . ."

Wide-awake now, Polly pulled the blanket up to her neck as she scanned the room. She had no idea where she was, and she recognized none of her surroundings. She turned her head in the opposite direction, to the other side of the bed, where she found herself face-to-face with Sky Captain.

From his bare shoulders—and especially from his mischievous grin—she guessed he was also naked. "Good morning, Polly."

She yelped. "What are you doing? Get out of here! *Get out!*"

He didn't move from the bed. Instead, he crossed his arms behind his head and lay back on the pillow. "Not unless you've got a pair of pants hidden under there. But I doubt it." His eyes twinkled. "Trust me, I already checked . . . thoroughly."

Polly's eyes moved down Sky Captain's concealed body, mortified. She tried to figure out some way to escape. "You're not . . . ?"

"Naked? You can say it, Polly. For a plucky reporter, you seem to have trouble with certain words."

"This isn't funny, Joe! What happened to us? Where are we? Who took our clothes?" Those were only the first few questions, but she could think of plenty more.

Sky Captain smiled impishly. Self-conscious, Polly pulled the blanket closer against her own bare skin. "You're enjoying this! Stop looking at me like that."

"Like what?"

"Turn around, Joe. I'm not kidding. Turn around. Look the other way."

Rolling his eyes, Sky Captain gave in. "Fine, fine."

With a weary noise, he rolled over to the other side of the bed, where he found himself staring at Kaji. The burly Sherpa was also naked and staring back at him. "Hi, Captain Joe."

Sky Captain barely had time to huddle under the covering again when the room's carved wooden door swung open. Sky Captain, Polly, and Kaji spun about, each holding the edge of the blanket tight to the neck.

An imposing Kalacakra priest with a painted face stood over them. He wore jewelry of beaten gold and polished stones, and his expression was both implacable and beatific. Polly didn't know if they were going to get more answers now . . . or just more questions.

Kaji moved his hands up to touch his forehead in silent greeting. As Sky Captain and Polly looked at him, the Sherpa nudged Sky Captain, who in turn elbowed Polly. Then Sky Captain and Polly touched their foreheads. The Himalayan priest looked at Sky Captain's bewildered face and smiled faintly.

Polly turned to Kaji, whispering past Sky Captain on the bed, "Ask him what they did with our clothes."

When the priest responded to Kaji's query, Kaji translated the other man's answer. "He says our clothes were burned."

"Burned? Why?" Polly cried.

"And that was my best leather jacket!" Sky Captain said.

After another incomprehensible exchange, Kaji said, "He says the mine is poisonous, that our clothes were infected. Even his magic could not purify them."

Sky Captain muttered, "The background radiation."

Three more priests entered the room, carrying new clothes in neatly folded piles and plates of fresh, colorful food from the orchards and gardens of Shangri-La.

Kaji continued. "He says they have arranged for a special porter to lead us back down the mountain, to where we belong. He will take us there once we have dressed."

Sky Captain acknowledged the priest, but spoke to Kaji. "Tell him we appreciate his offer, and everything he's done so far, but explain to him that we're looking for a man. That's what brought us here."

Kaji spoke to the priest, who gave a brusque answer before turning to the carved wooden door. The Sherpa looked sadly at Sky Captain. "He insists that we must leave before dark, that there is nothing more he can do for us."

The Kalacakra priest stepped through the door, not

interested in looking at the three outsiders again, but Sky Captain sat up in the bed. "Tell that priest it's very important we find him."

Kaji translated quickly, but the priest continued through the door and started to swing it shut.

"Tell him the man's name is *Totenkopf*."

The painted priest froze in his tracks, reacting to the word. "Totenkopf?" Slowly, he fixed an ominous gaze on Sky Captain.

The priest spoke sharply, and Kaji translated. "He asks what you want with this man."

Sky Captain leaned forward, not caring that the blanket fell down to his waist. He looked at the priest, intense. "I've come to kill him."

The Kalacakra priest looked at Sky Captain, but his painted face betrayed no emotion. Kaji translated again when the man finally spoke. "Then he says he will help you."

21

A Shortage of Film
A Forbidden Paradise
Slaves of Totenkopf

Later, still feeling refreshed, Sky Captain stepped out onto a balcony of the ornate citadel where they were held. He drew a deep breath of the electric mountain air. He had dressed in khakis and a leather jacket. He didn't ask where the denizens of this secret place had gotten such garments.

A silvery waterfall cascaded in the distance. Lush greenery framed his view. "Shangri-La . . ." Sky Captain didn't think he could stop smiling if he tried.

He turned upon hearing a sound behind him. Polly stepped through an arching doorway, dressed in an ornate Nepalese gown. She looked awkward, though she tried to pretend it was grace. "Well? What do you think, Joe?" She raised her arms and twirled, modeling the dress for him.

Sky Captain responded with a teasing frown. "I think they burned the wrong clothes."

Polly crossed her arms over her chest. "You told me I couldn't bring anything else."

He continued to inspect the heavy cloth of her garment, pursing his lips. "What is that anyway? Some kind of horse blanket?"

"I think it's beautiful."

"You look like a woolly mammoth."

"You're an idiot."

Smiling, he brushed past her. "It'll have to do, if that's all you've got to wear. Come on. They're waiting for us."

Not knowing if he was teasing or serious, Polly followed him.

Sky Captain, Polly, and Kaji strolled along beside the painted Kalacakra priest through a garden path that cut through the center of the village. The outsiders feasted their eyes on the grandeur of the place, overwhelmed by the strangeness.

Remembering her job as a reporter, Polly withdrew her camera, ready to document the amazing scenery of Shangri-La. "No one in the civilized world has ever seen anything like this." But when she checked the camera's exposure counter, her face went white.

"This can't be happening. I only have two shots left! I used up the rest of the pictures during our flight across the Himalayas, and my spare rolls of film were destroyed in the explosion! Everything I had was in that bag." She glared at Sky Captain. "You should have let me go back for my film!"

"You're right. I should have," he said, annoyed.

Polly stared forlornly at her camera. "We're in Shangri-La, and all I have is two shots!" In a daze, she continued walking behind the priest through the garden path.

Sky Captain whispered to Kaji, "That priest looks even grimmer than usual. Where is he taking us?"

The Sherpa seemed uneasy. "To what remains of Totenkopf's laboratory."

Polly finally caught up. "Totenkopf was here? In Shangri-La?"

"I don't think they liked him very much," Sky Captain said.

The Kalacakra priest stopped and motioned to the

steep and narrow steps leading up to an ancient lama-sery. Polly, Sky Captain, and Kaji followed him up the marble stairway. Grief and anger filled the priest's painted face.

Polly kept close to Sky Captain as they stepped into what had once been a sacred place. Everywhere she looked around the ancient temple, she saw scars and signs of abuse, defaced carvings, beautiful architecture now augmented with thick cables, heavy equipment, and foreign technology. The holy lamasery had been forcibly converted into a makeshift laboratory.

A steel plate bearing the emblem of the winged skull had been torn from the wall and left to rust on the dusty floor. The priest muttered angrily, and Kaji cocked his ear to listen. "He says this place is now tainted. But eventually, they will make it pure again."

The remnants of the crude lab seemed as frozen in time as the heavy mining operation in the mountains. Glass retorts, burners, specimen chambers, and electrical generators had lain neglected for years. The remains of deformed skeletons were on stained operating tables, still strapped down. Their toothy jaws gaped open, twisted in agony. Rotting creatures hung suspended in oily fluids. Tubes ran from batteries into scum-clogged tanks.

The silence and the musty smell of death made Polly turn away. "What happened here?"

Kaji translated for the priest. "He says Totenkopf enslaved the people of Shangri-La, made them work in his mine outside the valley. It was a terrible time. The workers all became sick, because the rocks in the mine were poisonous." The Sherpa nodded wisely. "Captain Joe showed me on his Geiger counter."

Then he listened as the priest continued his story. "Those workers who did not die from the radiation in the mines were brought here for Totenkopf to study. He used them for his unspeakable experiments."

Sky Captain and Polly looked at the deformed skeletons sprawled on the dissection tables. She moved closer to him.

"Mercifully, they did not live long," Kaji said.

Sky Captain balled his fists in anger. "Where is he? Kaji, ask him where Totenkopf is. What happened to him?" From the dust and silence all around, it was clear the evil genius had not been here for some time.

"The priest does not know—only that Totenkopf has been gone for many years now." He swept his hands to indicate the horrific laboratory. "This tainted lamasery is all that remains of his terrible legacy."

Polly looked sharply at Sky Captain. "Joe, Totenkopf must have led us here on purpose. Even though this place isn't significant to his plans, he knew we'd come after Dex and bring the vials straight to him."

"He has them now. All we've done is buy him time," Sky Captain grumbled. He was already impatient to go.

"There has to be something more." Polly turned to Kaji. "Isn't there anyone left? There must be someone we can talk to."

The angry priest stared bleakly around the remnants of the lab, then fought back tears in his eyes as he spoke in Nepalese. Kaji relayed the message. "You are right, Miss Perkins. One man lives: the last of Totenkopf's slaves. Perhaps he can help."

Sky Captain looked directly at the priest in the dim chamber of horrors. "Take me to him."

Inside one of the small shelters in the valley, a low fire shed orange light and the aromatic smell of sweet smoke. Perched on a small table, an antique wind-up phonograph played a scratchy recording of a Marlene Dietrich song.

Night had fallen outside, and a glorious panorama of stars looked like a fortune of diamonds in the sky, undimmed by clouds or city lights. After a polite knock on the edge of the door, the Kalacakra priest pushed a cloth hanging aside and gestured the companions inside. A croaking sound from the shadows conveyed a rasping welcome.

Sky Captain ducked as he entered, glancing around in the firelight. In one corner a miserable old man lay stretched on a modest cot. Wrapped in a blanket, he kept himself in the gloom. He shuddered even though the fire warmed the dwelling. When the visitors came into the room, the old man turned to face the wall, hiding his features, as if he was ashamed or afraid.

The intense priest encouraged them to step over to the cot. He bent to touch a swollen, twisted hand resting on the wrinkled blankets covering the old man's chest.

Polly knelt beside the cot, her face full of empathy and concern. Anxious to be after his quarry, Sky Captain turned to Kaji. "Ask him if he knows what happened to Totenkopf. Tell him it's important we find him. If he's the last survivor of the mine, maybe he knows something."

While the priest stood watching, Kaji bent over the huddled old man and spoke. After a moment a faint, weak voice replied. The words sounded watery, as if the man's lungs had dissolved.

The Sherpa seemed ill at ease as he replied. "He wants to know why . . . why do you seek Totenkopf?"

Sky Captain squared his jaw. "Tell him I've come to make Totenkopf pay for what he's done. To stop him from ever doing this again." Though the old man heard the steely determination in the pilot's voice, he refused to show himself in the orange firelight.

Kaji bent closer to the cot with clear reluctance, but he repeated Sky Captain's promise. After a moment, with a pain-racked wheeze, the gnarled form lifted a crippled hand. He extended a finger that looked like the branch of a wind-bent pine. He pointed toward the corner, where a short walking staff leaned against the wall.

"His cane? Is he asking for his cane?" Sky Captain took a step to retrieve it.

On his cot, the wretch continued to speak in a barely audible wheeze. Kaji translated as best he could. "He says to follow . . . Rana. That staff will lead you there. It will lead you to Totenkopf."

Sky Captain lifted the cane, turning it under the firelight, but he remained puzzled. Polly leaned close, also curious. The staff was unremarkable, about three feet long and topped with a T-shaped handle. The wood was dark and smooth, polished from years of palm sweat.

He turned to Kaji. "*Rana*? I don't understand. Tell him I don't understand."

Kaji tried again, but shook his head. "He says the same thing, Captain Joe. 'Follow Rana to the great cliffs of Bajarin. The staff will lead you.' "

"That doesn't make any sense." Sky Captain sifted through his knowledge, remembering all the terrain maps and nautical charts he had memorized over the years. Even at that time, in the twentieth century, much of the Himalayan plateau remained a question mark of geography. Shangri-La was mysterious and secret, but at least he had heard of it.

But . . . Rana? The great cliffs of Bajarin? "There's no such place," Sky Captain said.

The old man began to speak again, mumbling something barely audible. He sounded more urgent, desperate. Kaji turned to Sky Captain and Polly. "I can't get him to explain further. However, the man says now that he has helped you, you must do something for him. Something important."

"Of course. Anything." With a determined expression, Sky Captain leaned close to the man on the shadowy cot. "What do you want of me?"

With a surprisingly swift motion, the old wretch

reached out and grabbed the pilot's leather jacket, desperately pulling Sky Captain closer. The last survivor of Totenkopf's mines held on to him and raised himself into the light.

Polly gasped, and Sky Captain could only stare. The old man no longer looked human. His face had been twisted like a mask made of melted wax. His eyelids sagged. His lips hung open and he drooled thick greenish spittle. The monster's forehead was sunken as if his skull had half-dissolved, and breath whistled in and out of three craterlike nostrils. On the horribly disfigured face, Sky Captain saw an unending nightmare of pain and suffering.

With an inhuman warbling voice, the man gasped urgently in Sky Captain's ear. He didn't need Kaji to translate the old man's morbid plea: *"Kill me."*

22

A Star to Steer By
A Destination Revealed
The Point of No Return

Leaving Shangri-La behind, Sky Captain took to the air again. As his P-40 raced across the frozen lake at the base camp, gaining takeoff speed, the landing gear kissed the ice one last time and then the plane rose into the sky.

From the ground, Kaji waved good-bye with his mittened hands, and Sky Captain signaled back by tilting the plane's wings. In the rear of the cockpit, Polly hung on.

The Warhawk soared over the snowy peaks of the Himalayas. Sunlight glinted off the breathtaking landscape. Polly and Sky Captain sat quietly, surrounded by the low hum of the engine. Despite the awesome view, neither of them was interested in sightseeing.

In the back, Polly held the wooden staff the hideous wretch had given them. She turned it in her hands, feeling the polished surface and looking for clues. Despite their urgings, the old man had not been able to give them any useful information. The unusual staff seemed a futile tool for finding Totenkopf—or for rescuing Dex.

Polly brought the staff closer, trying to decipher strange markings. "Joe, did you look at this?"

"I looked at it, Polly. It's a stick."

"Not if you look *closely*." She ran her index finger along the staff, touching the little notches with her nail. "It's got marks on it. Very precise. Like a ruler." She inspected the T-shaped top of the staff and discovered two faint engraved pictures. "And there's a moon carved here and a picture of a star. The symbols must mean something. Can they guide us to this place he called Rana?"

Sky Captain drew a quick breath and clapped a hand to his forehead. "*Rana*, of course! I was so focused on maps and destinations that I didn't think of the obvious!" He grinned as he remembered the line from a John Masefield poem: *And all I ask is a tall ship and a star to steer her by . . .*

Sky Captain was suddenly all business. "A star! The old man wasn't describing a place. He was describing a star. In their mythology and astronomy, *Rana* is a star. That's it."

Polly leaned forward, affected by his excitement and hope. After their bickering and the hurtful things they had said to each other, she was glad to feel this shared moment of closeness.

As he casually monitored the cockpit controls, he remained oblivious to her, working out the puzzle in his mind. "Ancient sailors used to navigate by the night sky. They could determine their position by the moon and the stars." He reached over his shoulder to take the staff from Polly. There was barely room for her to hand him the stick in the crowded cockpit.

Guiding the plane with one hand, he studied the staff with newfound interest. "The Vikings were known to create maps for certain stars, latitude tables that required a key to decipher them. They called the key a Jacob's Staff." He lifted the old man's cane, looking over his shoulder to show Polly. "This has to be the key. That's why it was so important to him."

Sky Captain shifted his legs to gain more room in the front of the cockpit so that he could manage to hold the staff up to one eye like a wooden telescope. When he pulled the T-shaped handle toward him, an inner shaft extended from the main stick, moving freely like a trombone slide. "Very sophisticated! Why didn't we notice this before?" He made a scornful noise at himself. "Because I thought those people were just primitives in an uncivilized land—that's why."

As he studied the symbols and graduated markings, Polly also grew excited. "You mean this can really work? We can find Totenkopf—and Dex—with that thing?"

The plane flew along, drifting only slightly in the high air currents. The entire vault of the sky was empty, all theirs to explore. After glancing up to make sure their heading was steady, Sky Captain rummaged through the document pouches beside his left leg. He pulled out his navigation charts and a copy of *The Nautical Almanac*. "Ah, here's what I need."

Polly was surprised it would be so easy. "You can just look up the position of Rana?"

He held up the book. "We do it a little different now. All we needed to know was where to look."

The Warhawk soared along, guided by the new autopilot system Dex had installed. During the long journey from the Flying Legion base to the Himalayas, Sky Captain had made good use of the system. Now, the autopilot allowed him the time and concentration to figure out his navigation problem.

He unfolded a map and spread it on the cockpit gauges in front of him. He rested a small notebook on his knee, scribbling calculations in pencil." Using the Karakal Plateau as our assumed position"—he paused to consult the *Almanac*—"Rana is at latitude twenty degrees forty minutes. Right ascension zero three hours, forty-three minutes. Declination ten degrees six seconds." Using his fingers and a straight edge, Sky Captain drew a line across the center of the map. He double-checked his calculations, then smiled as he circled the end point of the line. "There it is."

Polly leaned close to see, but the line did not cross any land. The chart showed only an endless expanse of water. "There's nothing there, Joe. Are you sure you did it right?"

"Yes, I'm sure." He stared at the map. "If the old man was right, then Totenkopf is *here*. Dead center in the middle of nowhere."

"Sounds appropriate, I guess."

Neither of them wanted to suggest that the disfigured old wretch, poisoned and tormented after years of slavery inside the radiation-contaminated mines, might have been delirious, misguided . . . or just wrong.

Sky Captain drew a second line parallel to the first, only half the length of the other line. His shoulders slumped. "Remember, you were worried about running out of film for your camera?" He circled the end point of the shorter line. "It seems we've got a worse problem."

"Why?" Polly looked at the chart, curious. "What's that point mean?"

"That's where we run out of fuel." He began to sort through a series of charts. "The point of no return."

"The point of crashing into the ocean, you mean." She couldn't see the fuel gauge behind the scattered charts and maps. "And where are we now?"

"Almost on empty."

Alarmed, Polly sat back. "So what do we do? How do we get all the way to Totenkopf's base?"

Sky Captain's face remained an expressionless mask as he studied his charts, trying to think of a solution. Then a smile blossomed on his face. "Ah! Franky."

"Who?" Polly said.

"Franky Cook, an old buddy of mine." From the pouch at his feet, Sky Captain selected another map and spread it out on top of the first. "Runs a mobile reconnaissance outpost for the Royal Navy. Top secret, but it can't be more than a few hundred miles from here."

Polly tried not to show her relief. She still couldn't see the P-40's fuel gauge, though she thought the droning engines had begun to sound the slightest bit unsteady. "That'll do the trick."

Sky Captain shuffled the charts away from his cockpit controls and flipped open a small metal covering that hid a telegraph key. "If I can get a message to them, I might be able to arrange a rendezvous at those coordinates." Briskly, he tapped the key, sending out the clear and familiar tones of Morse code. When he finished his brief transmission, he flexed his fingers, then began the rapid-fire signaling again.

"What if they don't get the message?" Polly asked. "You're cutting it awfully close."

Briefly, Sky Captain thought about commenting that the extra weight of a certain uninvited female reporter had cut down on the distance the Warhawk could fly, but he kept his words to himself.

"Franky's never let me down. They'll be there." He could feel Polly looking at him with deep skepticism, so he repeated, "They'll be there."

23

Running on Empty
Manta Station
An Attack in the Clouds

An hour later, Sky Captain consulted the map that filled the small cockpit. He remained calm and brusque, but he couldn't hide his anxiety. Luckily, the paper charts obscured the warning indicator light on his fuel gauge. He checked his bearings, verified the plane's position, and peered into the cloud-studded expanse, searching. He did not see what he was looking for.

So close that he could feel her warm breath on his neck, Polly leaned forward to see the cockpit controls. One of the maps slid askew in the bumpy turbulence, and she spotted the warning indicator light. The gas-level needle had dipped far into the red. "Is that light supposed to be on?"

"*Now* you're worried about fuel?" he muttered. "Why didn't you think of that in Nanjing before cutting my line?"

She didn't hear him over the sputtering drone of the engine. "What did you say?"

"I said relax, Polly." He bit off his words, sounding anything but confident. "Everything's fine." As if to prove him wrong, the indicator light began to flash insistently, and the annoying buzz of an alarm began to sound. He tapped the gauge, as if that might change the reading. "Damn."

"We're out of fuel, aren't we?"

The P-40 lurched, and the engine began to cough. Sky Captain adjusted his controls, trying to coax just a little more distance out of the trusty airplane. "Don't bother me right now."

"I just asked a question." Polly wanted to pound the back of his chair. "Can't anything ever be simple with you?"

With a final sputter, the plane's engine went dead. An avalanche of silence blanketed them, broken only by the faint whistle of wind, the rattle of the fuselage, and Polly's very audible gulp. The plane's nose dipped downward in its steady fall. The propellers spun just a few more times, then froze in place.

Sky Captain worked the rudders, raising the wing flaps on the wings in an attempt to level the plunging aircraft. The Warhawk descended rapidly through layers of cloud like a huge artificial condor.

"Buckle up, Polly."

"How can you be so nonchalant about—"

Hitting a zone of turbulent air streams, the plane shuddered violently and tossed her against one side of the cockpit. She stopped complaining and fastened her belt.

Sky Captain lifted his microphone. "Come in Manta Station, do you read me? Come in Manta Station."

A steady hiss of static was his only reply.

"Where are you, Franky?" he said under his breath. "I could use a little reassurance right now."

Another bone-rattling bump, and Sky Captain pulled back on the controls with all his strength, forcing the plane to tilt upward as he caught a rising air mass.

As the P-40 shifted position, a loose glass bottle

rolled across the floor, stopping at Polly's feet. She looked down to see Sky Captain's milk of magnesia. With a quick glance at him, she grabbed the bottle and took a healthy swig, then wiped the chalky liquid from her lips. The taste was awful, and it didn't do much to settle her stomach.

"All right." Sky Captain reached for a lever. "I'm activating the landing gear." With a whirring thump and a locking click, the wheels came down in the underbelly and snapped into place.

"Landing gear?" Polly watched, stupefied. The disorienting clouds were all around them, and she couldn't see a thing, but she knew from the charts that they had no chance of finding any dry land. "Joe, what are you doing? You can't land this thing on the water."

"We're not landing on the water." Sky Captain hunched over the control panel, still trying to guide the falling airplane.

When they suddenly pierced the cloud coverage, Polly's face went white, but Sky Captain smiled calmly.

"We're landing on that," he said. It was a technological island in the sky, a huge metal-and-glass fortress held aloft by giant rotors that spun like giant fan blades. Guidance propellers and dangling rudders moved the levitating base to keep it hidden in the smokescreen of clouds. A complex of rectangular buildings formed a conning tower on one end of the station. The flag of the Royal Navy flew from a pole at the highest point.

Polly stared in wonder at the incredible flying fortress. "What is it?"

"A mobile airstrip. Dex helped design it, but the whole idea is kind of a secret." His voice became more deliberate. "You *can* keep a secret, can't you, Polly?"

"Yes, I can keep a secret . . . though it won't do

me much good if we crash before we can land on that thing." Out of sight behind him in the cockpit, Polly surreptitiously raised her camera to take a picture, then lowered it with a sigh of regret. "Two shots left . . ."

It seemed that every place she went with Joe Sullivan, the experience became more and more amazing. How was she supposed to choose the most newsworthy photographs? Editor Paley would probably lecture her for hesitating, but she couldn't waste her only two pictures.

A businesslike voice spiced with a thick British accent came over the cockpit radio. "This is Manta Station transmitting. Permission granted to land on platform three-two-seven. Maintain your present course."

"Copy!" His voice held a truckload of relief. "Three-two-seven. I'll be there."

"Welcome aboard, Captain Sullivan, sir."

Sky Captain expertly guided the Warhawk between the mammoth rotors, aligning his course with painted marks on the runway beneath him. With the remnants of his momentum and control, he cruised over the landing strip, struggling not to descend too rapidly. Polly cinched her seat belt tighter only a moment before the plane struck the airstrip hard. The landing gear bounced once, then again. Blue smoke curled from the brakes as the plane screeched to a bumpy stop.

Sky Captain slid open the canopy, filling the cockpit with fresh, chill air. Beaming, he stood up and waved, as if he made such desperate landings every day. He swung over the canopy edge and hopped down onto the deck of the flying fortress.

Uniformed British naval officers ran briskly from the support buildings at the base of the conning tower. After a glance behind him to see that Polly could get out of the plane unassisted, Sky Captain stepped up to meet the small welcoming committee.

In the lead of the group, a statuesque beauty with a distinct air of sophistication came forward. She wore a dark uniform, neat and perfect; under her Royal Navy cap, her dark hair was bound up per regulations. A black patch covered her right eye, hinting at a past as adventurous as Sky Captain's. She stopped to inspect him with wry skepticism, looking at his bullet-riddled plane. Her generous lips quirked in a cool smile.

"Well, Joseph Sullivan, I thought for sure you'd be dead by now."

"I might have been, if you weren't here." After a brief pause, Sky Captain threw open his arms. He and the lovely commander of the flying fortress embraced earnestly like old war buddies. "It's good to see you, Franky!"

Neither of them paid any attention to Polly as she climbed down the side of the Warhawk. Polly flinched with an inadvertent jealous pang. "Franky? *This* is Franky?" She brushed the wrinkles from her clothes, felt her legs tingling and numb from being bent in the back of the little cockpit. Then she hurried forward.

Sky Captain and Franky let their hug linger just a moment too long. Ignoring Polly, the woman stepped back to inspect Sky Captain's rumpled appearance. "This had better be important, Joseph, or one of us is in trouble."

"Oh, it's important. Trust me."

Franky glanced over at Polly, raising her eyebrows. "Who's the girl? Excess baggage?"

Remembering his manners, Sky Captain made awkward introductions. "Uh, Captain Francesca Cook, meet Polly Perkins, reporter for the New York *Chronicle*."

The two women squared off coolly with Sky Captain

standing between them. "Oh, yes, Polly Perkins . . . I've heard so much about you." Franky formally extended her hand, and the two shook, but without warmth. "It's a pleasure to finally meet my competition."

Stunned by the female captain's beauty and cultured manner, Polly felt inadequate and self-conscious. Franky had heard so much about her? What had Joe been saying? Polly doubted it was overcomplimentary.

Done with the pleasantries, Franky turned all her attention back to Sky Captain. Her voice was full of innuendo. "It's been a long time since Nanjing, Joseph."

Nanjing? Polly flashed Sky Captain an accusing glare. He became flustered, but tried to hide it. "Yes, a long time." After an awkward silence, he yanked off his flying gloves and briskly rubbed his hands together. "So, well . . . how's that number three engine, Franky? Dex always thought it was wobbly, and I remember it running a little rough—"

Suddenly a warning Klaxon assaulted their ears. Flashing lights strobed up and down the flying fortress's runways. A voice boomed over loudspeakers mounted on the rotor towers. "General quarters! Man your battle stations. All hands on deck!"

The emergency distracted both Polly and Franky. "Thank God," Sky Captain said under his breath.

A uniformed officer bounded across the runway, waving a piece of paper at Franky. "Commander! We're tracking six enemy submersibles, bearing thirty degrees northwest."

"Most unusual. Do you recognize the configuration?"

"No, Commander. Not a design we've encountered before. The submersibles are very large, and they seem to be heavily armed." The young officer hesitated. "There are indications that they may have spotted us already."

Franky raised her eyebrows at Sky Captain again. "Who wants to kill you this time, Joseph?"

He flushed. "Oh, you know, it's always something."

A large explosion erupted in the clouds around them, so close that it rocked Manta Station. The rotors hummed more loudly, stabilizing the airborne runway. Royal Navy crewmen ran to their posts, yelling orders.

The sky filled with flak fire. Echoes of successive detonations cracked like a thunderstorm through the cloud cover. It seemed like the grand finale of a fireworks display, and the flying fortress was right in the middle of it.

24

An Island out of Nowhere
Undersea Machines
A Grim Incentive

One of the blasts came close enough to tilt the station's vast deck, throwing Polly off balance, but Sky Captain instinctively caught her. The giant propellers strained to lift the heavy platform higher into the safety of the clouds. Franky shouted orders, but her well-trained crew already knew what to do.

Through hatches in the flying fortress's deck, Royal Navy gunners climbed down ladders into upside-down turrets hanging from structures beneath the platform. Large-caliber cannons extended as the men strapped into their seats. They let loose a roaring barrage to bombard the unseen enemies far below.

Sky Captain looked forlornly at his Warhawk, which sat motionless at the end of long black skid marks. "Franky, how fast can your people refuel my plane and load up?"

"Not fast enough, Joseph. Follow me. Right this way."

Hurrying, but showing no panic, Franky led them into the bridge structure. Sky Captain grabbed the edge of the door as another blast rocked the platform, and Polly went sprawling. Franky simply rode it out without losing her balance. "It'll take a while for you both to acquire your sea legs. Needs a bit of practice."

During the emergency, the bridge was a circus of organized chaos. Naval officers stood at their stations, shouting rapid-fire instructions and responses. Fighter pilots checked in as they sprinted across the various runways to scramble aboard their planes. Outside, louder than the constant thunder of explosions, dozens of aircraft engines fired up, propellers whirring, exhausts roaring. From the gun turrets below, defensive fire continued from the hull-mounted artillery.

Sky Captain marched close to Franky as if he belonged at her side, and Polly did not let him get too far ahead. Franky stepped up to her executive officer inside the command station. "I'll take over from here, Major Slater."

"Yes, Commander." He seemed relieved to relinquish control.

Sweeping her glance across the stations, Franky assessed their situation. "First order of business: raise us to ten thousand feet and deploy all countermeasures." The executive officer swiftly repeated her orders to the appropriate personnel.

Franky stood with perfect posture. In a piece of polished metal on one of the bridge stations, Polly spotted her own disheveled reflection and grimaced. "I don't appear to be much competition at all."

Franky went to a tactical table and spread out a map of the vicinity below. She motioned for Sky Captain to join her, and the two of them huddled over the charts. Their heads were very close together. Polly strained on her tiptoes, trying to peek over their shoulders.

Franky used a slender finger to point out an area where someone had drawn handwritten notes and a question mark on a blank expanse of ocean. "Right about here, Joseph. Our reconnaissance located a small island three kilometers northeast of our current position. It's not on any of our charts."

Polly couldn't contain her excitement. "That has to be him!"

Franky looked up, quizzical; she seemed to have forgotten the other woman was behind them. "Sorry? Has to be who?" She directed her question to Sky Captain, pointedly ignoring Polly. "What did you get me into this time, Joseph?"

His smile looked a bit too admiring. "Oh, it's nothing you can't handle, Franky."

Their calm camaraderie and respect made Polly wonder again just how deep this friendship went. Her brow furrowed.

Though the flying fortress was gaining altitude, lifted aloft by the churning propellers, one of the enemy missiles slammed into the bottom of the hull. Sparks flew from two control stations, and the level floor tilted at a severe angle.

Seasick, Polly grabbed an instrument panel and held on for her life, but as she clutched the controls, she accidentally yanked a lever. One of the rotors roared with increased power output, and Manta Station tilted in the opposite direction. She felt as if she were trapped on a giant seesaw in the sky.

Sky Captain lurched over and pointedly lifted her hand off the lever. "*Try* not to touch anything. In case you haven't noticed, we're in the middle of an emergency here."

Franky worked at a different station to stabilize the flying fortress. The commander flashed a glare with her one eye.

Polly sniffed. "I didn't mean to." Explosions continued to pepper the sky. The unending Klaxon sound was giving her a headache.

With the flying fortress rising steadily again on a stable course, Franky stepped up behind a young ensign manning a sonar array. A pattern of bright blips crossed the display screen, blurred outlines like ghosts in the fog. "Ah, so there you are."

"Commander!" the executive officer called. "Enemy warships, bearing three-one-six, mark four. Closing fast." He studied his own screen. "They're coming into firing range. We're about to have a spot of trouble, I believe."

Franky strode over to uniformed engineers at a communications array. "Give me a visual please."

The communications engineer activated a series of dials and switches. "Yes, Commander. Launching radio imager."

After he depressed a button, bat-wing hatches beneath the flying fortress opened and dropped a tiny beeping probe. It tumbled through the sky, falling past explosions, gunfire, and clouds of dissipating smoke, until it splashed like a small torpedo beneath the waves. Automated systems kicked in, and the probe turned about, orienting itself in the depths. Its sensors and range finders targeted a group of hulking shadows that cruised underwater.

"We're receiving a signal on-screen now, Commander," said the communications engineer. "Here comes the telemetry."

Sky Captain, Franky, and Polly stood together watching a small circular display. On the curved glass screen, a school of fleeing fish streaked past. Then a crude blurry image slowly resolved into a startling picture.

Twenty gargantuan iron machines emerged from the murk. The sea-bottom walkers plodded along like giant crabs, each with four massive segmented legs. They scuttled in inexorable slow motion, stirring up silt and mud from the ocean floor with every ponderous step.

With its next signal, the radio imager finally broadcast a clear picture of the winged-skull emblem on the foremost sea-bottom walker. "Totenkopf," Polly said, stating the obvious.

Then the crab machines' angular carapaces opened. With a gush of foam and flame, blunt rockets emerged, churning up to the target in the sky.

"They're still firing at us!" the executive officer shouted.

An explosive shell ripped through the flying fortress's deck, plowing through girders and thick hull plates before it detonated. Smoke and fire curled upward, stirred by the valiantly churning rotors. Debris showered down. Alarms and emergency signals ricocheted around the bridge.

Franky finally had the good grace to look flustered. "I believe I've had enough of this." She turned to the pilot. "All engines reverse full. Get us out of here. My apologies, Joseph, but I have no choice but to retreat. The better part of valor and all that."

Sky Captain staggered to the chart table and looked down at the map, determined. "Franky, you've got to get me onto that island."

She did not seem amused. "You don't ask for much, do you?"

An undersea crab walker fired another volley of explosive rockets. Detonations rocked the flying fortress, ripping a huge hole through the armored deck. Now smoke began to fill the conning tower. Emergency crews ran about, spraying fire extinguisher foam.

"Commander, we've lost power in the forward rotors! We're losing altitude!" said the executive officer. They could all feel the stomach-lurching plunge as Manta Station began to fall.

Polly grabbed for something to keep her balance. She was careful not to bump any controls this time.

Franky shook her head. "I'm very sorry, Joseph. You know I've never said no to you, but it's impossible. If we stay here any longer, we're dead—"

Sky Captain gazed into her single bright eye, giving

the only explanation that mattered: "He's got *Dex*, Franky."

She looked at him, suddenly understanding. He had known that would be the trump card for Franky Cook.

Dexter Dearborn Jr. had developed Manta Station after reading a Jules Verne novel called *Clipper of the Clouds*. At first glance, the design had made no aerodynamic sense at all, but Dex had insisted on it. Then he built models and proved his idea would work. Franky Cook had taken a great risk to support the young genius, advocating the strategic importance of flying runways that could deliver a squadron of aircraft to any battlefield in the world.

And Dex had not let her down. He had overseen the construction of Manta Station, checked all the engineering himself, and flown on the maiden voyage. The young man had managed to endear himself to Franky, just as he had done with the rest of the Flying Legion.

Sky Captain knew that Dex had an impossible crush on the lovely Royal Navy captain. He found the thought of it amusing, but Franky actually seemed to take the young man's advances seriously. She did owe him her life and her career, after all.

On the huge station's second flight, Dex had been uneasy just from listening to the engines. He'd nosed around in the casing for the number three engine, though it had repeatedly passed inspection. At the last moment, though, Dex found a saboteur's bomb and deactivated it, preventing the destruction of the flying fortress and saving the lives of everyone aboard.

Yes, Franky Cook would take any necessary risks to rescue him now.

"Commander!" the executive officer called.

She no longer seemed to hear the continuing explosions around them. "Do whatever you must, Major Slater, but get this platform stabilized. We've got work to do—serious work."

Not noticing or caring about anything else, Franky and Sky Captain bent over the map with equal resolve. "Under this bombardment, you'll never make it to that island from the air, Joseph," she said. "We'll have to find another way in."

25

Another Way In
A Special Amphibious Squadron
Flying Comrades

Smoke continued to pour into the bridge station. Outside, the huge rotors roared in an attempt to keep the damaged flying fortress aloft, but the leviathan crab walkers continued to fire missile after missile out of the water.

Holding on to the chart table as detonations made them lurch from side to side, Franky and Sky Captain continued to scour the map for options. Behind them, Polly couldn't help feeling a jealous pang at seeing the other two work so closely as a team.

Sky Captain jabbed his finger on a discoloration marked on the chart. "Look here. There's a tidal flow along the eastern face of the island. Maybe we could—"

Franky shook her head, adjusting the neat cap atop her dark hair. "It's too deep. None of our vessels is rated past three hundred meters." She leaned closer. "Wait, this area here. . . ."

She yanked a clear overlay from the adjacent navigation table, placing it across the map of the ocean to match a crude hand-drawn outline of the newly discovered island. "We just spotted this with one of

Dex's sonar mapping probes." She paused, letting out a brief sigh. *Good old Dex*. Then she cleared her throat and continued. "There's an undersea inlet at the southern tip of the island here. It runs beneath the entire length of the island."

Just as she was using a grease pencil to mark an area on the map, the bridge took another hit, and a hammer blow of vibrations shuddered through the deck. Franky held the grease pencil so firmly, though, that her line showed only the tiniest fluctuation. "That's your only way in. Everything else is sheer rock to the edge of the water."

"But you saw the twenty crab walkers down there. What about them?" Polly had to raise her voice over the din of the continuing attack. "How do we get past those machines?"

With a tone of dismissal, Franky said, "Leave that to me." She turned to her executive officer and gave the order. "Major Slater, alert the amphibious squadron. In the meantime, Joseph, you'd better get your Warhawk ready."

The air around the smoking airborne base was a tapestry of tracer fire and diving aircraft. Fighter squadrons swarmed around the flying fortress, machine guns ratcheting as they intercepted the explosive rockets that climbed up to the vulnerable target. The turret gunners below the main framework continued to take aim, but deep water protected the submerged crab walkers. One of the gun turrets had been struck by a missile, leaving only a mangled framework of broken glass and melted struts to mark where a man had died.

On top, the flight deck was alive with activity. Over the wailing sirens and the roar of emergency equipment, loudspeakers summoned the Royal Navy's special operations forces. "Manta Team, report to main staging area! Manta Team, report to main staging area."

At a separate runway, circular hatches opened and elevated platforms rose from maintenance hangars beneath the runway. A row of strange-looking planes emerged into the open air. Each Manta vessel had a streamlined, sharklike appearance and camouflage marking in oceanic shades of blue. The canopy over each cockpit was a bubble of thick glass. Mirrored spotlights shone like eyes from the blunt noses of the craft; scooped propellers were mounted in the rear of the boomerang wings.

Royal Navy crewmen prepped the aircraft. Their precision movements demonstrated how often they drilled and trained for emergencies such as this. With a rattle of questions and responses, they raced through checklists in record time. The lead crewman waved a colored flashlight, signaling to one of the low buildings next to the conning tower. He whistled. "All ready!"

Emerging from the status room, a jumble of black-suited pilots raced down the narrow corridor. Shouting encouragement to one another, they charged into an equipment room, ready to go. They grabbed gloves, tanks, and air hoses. On a rack hung a long row of transparent bubble helmets that looked like fishbowls, each clearly marked with a person's name.

Once again, Dex had been influenced by Buck Rogers.

The pilots of the elite amphibious squadron had all been handpicked by Captain Francesca Cook. The unit was made up entirely of women.

The members of the Royal Navy's special underwater flying squadron wore identical black, formfitting flight suits—part bomber jacket and part scuba outfit, with a silver breathing apparatus secured to their backs. The clinging uniforms left no doubt as to the sex of the amphibious pilots.

Once suited up, the women wasted no time. They dashed to their waiting underwater planes and climbed inside. Crewmen helped seal the cockpit bubbles, checked to make sure they were airtight, then slapped the sides of the craft. Engines thrummed and powered up. The Manta vehicles levitated slightly, ready for takeoff. . . .

Men in grimy coveralls worked on the P-40, refueling and resupplying, patching the Warhawk just enough so that it could fly into battle again. Leaving the bridge of the flying fortress, Sky Captain and Polly ran to their plane, which sat where they'd left it, at the end of one short runway. "Polly, you should just stay here. It'll be safer."

Thunderous explosions continued to echo in the air. Debris from the aerial blasts pelted all around them, rattling off the fuselage of the P-40, but the plane did not appear to be damaged. "Really, Joe?"

"Get in, then."

Franky ran alongside them, determined to get to her own aircraft.

Reaching his Warhawk, Sky Captain yelled back over his shoulder, "Franky, are you sure this is ready to go?"

"It's in much better shape than when you arrived here, Joseph."

"That isn't saying a lot," Polly said, but nevertheless she swiftly situated herself in her familiar seat at the rear of the cockpit. Concussions struck all around them.

"Good luck, Joseph!"

Sky Captain waved at her, grinning. "Good luck to you too, Franky. Get us to that island, and we'll take care of Totenkopf."

As Franky settled inside her own plane and sealed the canopy, she adjusted her eye patch, then looked back at the P-40. She and Sky Captain exchanged the sort of exhilarating smile that only two pilots about to fly off into danger could possibly understand.

As he turned around to face the cockpit controls, Sky Captain noticed Polly's cool glare. "What?" he asked, suddenly self-conscious. *"What?"*

"Ahem . . . what did she say about Nanjing?"

Fastening his leather cap, Sky Captain pretended not to understand her. "Can't hear you, Polly. Too much background noise. You'll have to speak up."

Then he hit the ignition, and his engines roared to life.

26

Underwater Flight
War Stories
A Monstrous Guardian

When their engines were powered up and the propellers spun in a blur, both planes strained like horses at a gate, anxious to begin a race. At a joint signal, both Sky Captain and Franky took off, streaking along the newly pocked runway.

As they accelerated headlong toward the sudden drop-off at the edge of the flying fortress, Polly squeezed her eyes shut. Suddenly they were airborne, dropping away with a stomach-lurching descent. Now that his plane had been fueled and repaired, Sky Captain easily leveled them off, soaring away from the Royal Navy's secret island in the sky. "Piece of cake," he muttered.

Franky spoke into her headset as she soared ahead of him. "Mind your nose, Joseph. You were always bad on the short takeoff. This isn't like one of those sprawling runways you have groundside."

"Just try to keep up, Franky," Sky Captain said with a teasing lilt. "I don't want to have to come back for you."

"You never could take a bit of constructive criticism."

Behind him, Polly said gently, for his ears alone, "I thought your takeoff was fine."

Sky Captain turned appreciatively. "Thanks, Polly."

She seized on it. "Oh, so you heard *that*, did you?"

Sky Captain shot her a look of annoyance, then turned his attention back to the controls.

Immediately behind them, the amphibious squadron took to the air, a rapid succession of plane after plane leaping like fish off a dock. A quick burst of chatter filled the P-40's cockpit as female voices checked in from the elite underwater group. Their launch had been textbook perfect.

The Warhawk flew alongside Franky's craft, and the amphibious planes swooped in formation. All together, they dove at full speed toward the ocean below.

"Time for some sport, everyone," Franky said over the headset. Her voice remained rich, calm; she sounded as if she was in her perfect element. "Manta Leader to Manta Team, prepare for impact in ten seconds. Switching to amphibious mode."

Knowing the rest of the squadron was already following suit, Franky reached for a switch on her control panel. She could feel her aircraft shifting and adjusting all around her. A complex array of servomechanisms shifted plates and vents, locking down seals, preparing the plane for underwater flight.

When the transformation was complete, Franky saw the looming expanse of water rushing toward her. She and her special squadron had already made a hundred or more successful practice runs, but actual combat was so much more enjoyable. Her plane dove straight down. She called out the countdown. "Impact in five . . . four . . . three . . . two . . ."

Immediately beside her, as if it were some sort of choreographed water ballet maneuver, Sky Captain's Warhawk plunged into the waves. Behind them, the full squadron of amphibious planes dove into the water, vanishing beneath the surface, leaving only a scar of churned foam to mark where they had entered the sea.

The group of special aircraft descended through the cold murk until they began to glide along just above the ocean floor. They cruised silently along as they approached the secret island of Dr. Totenkopf.

Polly had already seen the P-40's special capability, but she still stared around herself at the eerie submerged landscape. Though they were far from the commercial shipping lanes, the silty sea bottom was strewn with the remains of sunken vessels. Apparently, any ship that passed too close to the mad genius's isolated stronghold became part of the watery graveyard.

Sky Captain looked out the side of the canopy as they passed over the hull of a massive, ancient ship, already covered with gauzy strands of brownish seaweed. Stenciled across the bow of the wreck, the name was barely readable: *VENTURE*.

Polly knew the attack was continuing overhead, and the flying fortress was fighting for survival, but for a moment the scenery around them seemed silent and calm, a much-needed respite after their long adventure—even with the wrecked ships all around.

Then Franky's voice came over the cockpit communication system, ruining the mood. "Joseph, do you remember that milk run over Shanghai? I was pulling the bus, and you had that *jerk* for a wingman."

"Right! We had the target buttoned up, and he was hedgehopping in that little kite, jinxing in the flak and taking quick squirts at foam." Sky Captain brightened, clearly happy to be reminiscing about old war stories.

Polly couldn't understand a thing they were saying.

Franky began to chuckle at the memory, as Sky Captain continued. "Pops a rivet, thinks he's taken a hit, and starts yelling in the radio—"

Franky joined him, and both started yelling in unison,

their voices a mock falsetto, " 'Protect the rabbits! Protect the rabbits!' " He convulsed with laughter.

Polly looked at him, bewildered. "What the hell was that all about?"

He lifted a gloved hand to wave her off. "It would take too long to explain, Polly—"

"Try me."

Before he could make up an excuse, the deep water around them was suddenly shattered by repeated explosions, depth charges or artillery launched from submarine guns. The shock waves threw them into turbulence much worse than anything Polly had ever felt in the air. As they rounded a stony canyon wall, explosive flak continued to buffet the crack squadron. Orange flashes and blossoms of white bubbles appeared all around them.

The radar screen on Sky Captain's control panel lit up, accompanied by an ominous beeping tone. "Proximity alarm. Something big . . . and probably dangerous."

Franky spoke over the underwater radio. "I'm picking up a sort of cavity on radar—four points to the right, depth sixteen hundred. Look sharp!" Together, the squadron searched the underwater landscape for their target.

Inside the Warhawk, Polly and Sky Captain spotted it at the same time, a dark and shadowy opening that looked like a dangerous cave, barely wide enough to accommodate the P-40's wingspan.

Franky signaled him. "Joseph, there's the inlet that leads beneath the island, as you requested. Told you I'd get you here."

"Does she have to sound so smug?" Polly said.

Sky Captain had already accelerated toward the forbidding cave. "I see it. We're on our way."

Franky's plane cruised in front of him, taking the lead. Before they could react, a camouflaged walking machine rose in front of the cave, larger than the other four-legged crab robots. Covered with barnacles and the shredded debris of other metal victims, the machine loomed until it towered over Franky's plane. Mammoth jointed arms reached up with huge sharp claws capable of ripping through the hull of a battleship. The giant crab machine completely blocked the way through the inlet.

"Franky, look out! Abort the run," Sky Captain shouted into the radio.

But the Royal Navy commander answered with a cool chuckle. "I never guessed you to be a man who would give up so easily, Joseph." She didn't decelerate at all. "And please don't underestimate my amphibious squadron."

The Manta underwater planes roared in after her, showing no hesitation. Sky Captain shrugged, then pushed the stick forward so his Warhawk could keep up. "All right."

Franky stared ahead through the swirling murk, hunched over her controls. Bubbles and submerged explosions made muffled echoes through the sealed walls of her modified plane, sounding like the drumbeats of a drowning percussion section.

The huge crablike robot grew larger and larger, extending razor-edged armor fins and waiting for Franky to come into reach. She did not show a hint of the awe that she felt. She clicked the microphone again. "Get ready to make a run for it, Joseph. We're going to clear you a path—for Dex."

"For Dex." Sky Captain looked behind him, catching a glimpse of Polly's grim nod. He drove his P-40 behind the clustered amphibious squadron. Like a locomotive, they charged toward the giant machine.

At the front of the squadron, Franky lined up the monstrosity in her crosshairs. Her fingers flipped a row of switches, and all systems answered with a comforting glow of ready lights. "Manta leader to Manta Team, cluster torpedoes and stick close to element formation."

A sequence of angry female voices responded with brusque acknowledgments.

Sky Captain watched as the squadron drew closer. The seconds seemed to pass with incredible slowness. "Hold on, Polly."

"Is this going to work, Joe?"

"If Franky's convinced, then I wouldn't dream of doubting her."

Polly wasn't comforted by his comment. Instead, she thought again of what a great story this was going to make for the *Chronicle* . . . if any of them survived. Even if she had only two pictures left in her camera.

"Steady . . . one more second." Franky's finger hovered over the trigger button on her flight stick. The crab robot launched missiles that exploded around her; she and her Manta squadron were moving too fast to make decent targets. The violent turbulence threw off her aim, but she centered the enemy robot again in the crosshairs. More depth charges seemed about to shake her plane apart. She raced headlong toward the four-legged machine. "Fire!"

Close around her on all sides, the amphibious squadron launched their wing-mounted torpedoes. Swirling contrails traced dozens of paths, all of which converged toward the underwater monster. They flew in, directly on target, like iron filings drawn to a huge magnet.

In rapid sequence, all the torpedoes impacted against the barnacle-covered hull, creating a series of speckled explosions. Unfortunately, the dense exoskeleton was proof against even the most powerful projectiles. The spangles of light were like no more than mosquitoes, and the mechanical monster shrugged them off as it continued forward.

The magnified shock waves swept backward, causing more difficulties for the oncoming underwater planes. The Manta craft scattered, then struggled to get back into formation.

Sky Captain grabbed the controls, fighting to keep his submerged Warhawk out of a wild spin that would crash him into the sunken wrecks. He pulled up just in time to avoid a direct impact against a jagged rock projection, an ages-old coral stalagmite rising like a barbarian's spear. The hull of the P-40 scraped the rough stone, breaking off the sharp point, which tumbled and spun backward until it lodged in his rudder.

They careened toward the yawning mouth of the undersea cave and the mechanical leviathan that guarded it. Warning alarms sounded inside Sky Captain's plane as he struggled in vain to guide it. The Warhawk would not respond. Sweat poured down his brow.

Polly clutched the back of the pilot's seat. "What is it, Joe?"

Sky Captain fought with his control stick, wrestling it from side to side, but the plane hurtled forward. "I can't steer. Something's jamming the rudder."

As debris and foam from the succession of torpedo detonations cleared, Sky Captain and Polly suddenly looked up to see the giant machine—undamaged— rearing up and extending its terrible claw arms.

Sky Captain was speeding straight for it, unable to control his plane. He had no way to stop.

Franky watched in horror as the Warhawk shot toward the crablike robot. The snarling jaws painted on the nose of his plane made him look like an attacking shark. She yelled into her cockpit microphone. "Joseph, disengage! Do you read me? Joseph!"

The crab monster settled back on its segmented rear legs, exposing the overlapping iron plates on its underbelly. A round weapon port opened, and a spurt of bubbles accompanied the release of a fast spearhead torpedo. The underwater rocket locked onto its target, accelerating toward Sky Captain's oncoming plane.

Polly cried out. "Joe, *look*!"

Still struggling to steer, Sky Captain could not swerve in time to avoid the torpedo. The plane's rudder wiggled, strained, but the broken rock shaft only wedged in tighter. "We're dead in the water," he said. "Literally."

The torpedo closed fast. . . .

final episode

"THE MYSTERIOUS DR. TOTENKOPF"

Aboard the flying fortress, Sky Captain and Polly have discovered the location of a mysterious island. . . .

Meanwhile, an enemy torpedo is heading straight for Sky Captain's Warhawk as he attempts to evade the island's defenses. . . .

27

Drawing Fire
A Desperate Ploy
A Narrow Escape

When the enemy torpedo was only seconds from hitting Sky Captain's crippled plane, Polly fought the instinct to squeeze her eyes shut. "Didn't Dex add extra armor to your plane, Joe? Might that . . . ?"

"It won't be enough," Sky Captain said, his voice heavy. "My only hope is that the explosion will wipe out the robot monster along with us. Then maybe Franky can finish the job."

"Oh, Joe . . ."

"Polly?" He sounded sincere, hesitant. She thought he wanted to tell her something meaningful.

The crab machine's torpedo was coming straight toward them. It was fifty yards away . . . twenty. . . .

Then Sky Captain said, "You should have taken your last two photos at Shangri-La."

At the last moment, Franky's plane plunged in front of the Warhawk, swooping so close that her stirring backwash nudged the P-40 out of the way. Her unexpected appearance was like a wild dog in a chicken coop, and as she raced past, her plane presented a closer and larger target for the torpedo's sensors. She drew the automated missile away from Sky Captain.

"Come on, then," Franky said with a forced chuckle, "let's follow the leader."

Even Polly cheered. Sky Captain laughed into his microphone. "Thanks, Franky. That was close."

But as she pulled the torpedo along in her wake, Franky had more in mind than just diverting the underwater rocket. With the swirling missile in close pursuit, she pushed her plane to its limits and made a tight arching loop. Flying upside down, she turned her aircraft back toward the lumbering crablike crawler at the mouth of the cave. Unshaken by the maneuver, the torpedo came fast on her tail.

"Get ready to make a run for it, Joseph," Franky's voice said over the cockpit speaker. "You're only going to have one shot at this."

"Franky, I'm not much use. My rudder's jammed. I can't—"

Franky's plane dove overhead on a collision course for the crab machine. "She's heading straight for it," Polly said. "On purpose."

"That lady doesn't do many things by accident." Sky Captain lifted his microphone, unable to keep the alarm out of his voice. "Franky, what are you doing? This is no time to show off." But there was no question in his mind about what she intended to do. "She's going to ram it."

"But that's suicide!" Polly said.

"It's her way of accomplishing a mission." His face paled. "Damn it, Franky, pull up!"

But her amphibious plane rocketed straight for the lumbering monster. She completed a half barrel roll, putting herself right side up again. The menacing torpedo followed, closing the gap.

"On my mark." Her voice was maddeningly calm. "Don't let me down, Joseph. I'm going to rather a lot of trouble for you here."

"Franky! *No!*" Sky Captain was horrified.

"Three . . ."

Even with her mixed emotions toward the beautiful and mysterious British captain, Polly was drawn in. She whispered under her breath, "No, Franky. You don't need to do it."

"Two . . ."

"Franky, pull up! Come on, pull up!"

"One . . ."

Now Polly closed her eyes.

The giant crab machine completely filled the view in front of Franky. The torpedo closed the few remaining feet at her tail, its proximity fuse triggered. Everything happened faster than the human eye could absorb.

Franky grabbed a lever on the cockpit roof, yanking it down with all her strength. A spark flashed, clamps disengaged, and a small charge detonated to augment tightly coiled springs beneath her padded chair. The cockpit canopy blasted away, and the newly installed ejector seat flung her up through the water.

Just below, the merest fraction of a second after she shot away, the torpedo struck the tail of her plane and detonated. At the same moment, her underwater aircraft, now empty, crashed at full speed into the looming crab monster.

It seemed that the whole ocean convulsed with the terrific explosion. Shock waves slammed upward, nipping at Franky's heels as her ejector seat burst free of the wave tops like the cork from a shaken bottle of champagne. Shoved back with the force of the launch, Franky rode it through a rush of foam, gripping the arms of her chair. Beneath her, the sea roiled from the underwater fury. It was quite a ride.

As soon as she reached the open air, before the pilot seat ascended to the zenith of its trajectory, a rotor system activated under her seat. Slender alloy blades unfurled and began to spin, carrying her safely upward like an inverted version of Igor Sikorsky's new "helicopter" craft.

The previously untried escape system worked like a charm. "Thanks again for your imagination, Dex." She looked across to the misty silhouette of the nearby mysterious island. "Once you get rescued, I promise I'll buy you a year's subscription to any pulp magazine you like."

The rest of the Royal Navy's special amphibious squadron breached the surface of the waters below, activated their air engines, and rose from the ocean. Franky used controls in her chair to guide her own ascent. Together, they climbed toward the relative safety of the damaged flying fortress. . . .

After the explosion, Sky Captain's Warhawk sailed through the watery inferno. The cauldron of bubbles and half-vaporized debris from the ruined crablike robot battered them like a whirlwind and dislodged the jammed stalactite in the P-40's rudder. The controls suddenly moved in his grip.

"Hey, I can maneuver again!"

The Warhawk rode the choppy waters past the sagging hulk of the destroyed guardian, and they finally slipped inside the undersea inlet.

The cockpit radio crackled to life with the familiar voice of Franky Cook transmitting from her ejected seat. "You're all clear, Joseph. Good luck. Go save Dex."

"Thanks, Franky. We'll take it from here." Relieved to hear she had escaped, he clicked off the radio. His plane plunged deeper into the cave.

Polly was unable to deny her exhilaration. "That Franky's some kind of girl."

"Yeah, I know," Sky Captain said.

28

An Underwater Passage
A Remarkable Jungle
A Land That Time Forgot

Always alert for more of Totenkopf's monstrous defenses, the Warhawk drifted through the underwater cave, following bends and curves in the inlet. The plane's engine droned with a low hum, muffled by the murky water.

Spotlights emerged from the nose of the aircraft, shining into the mysterious labyrinth. Around them, the sheltered currents offered a strange tranquillity for a universe of bizarre sea life.

Polly pressed her face against the canopy glass like a small child, her eyes filled with wonder. All manner of exotic fish, mollusks, and honeycombed coral growths passed before them—things she had never seen in any aquarium or naturalist's book.

Prehistoric sea lilies with segmented stalks and hard clamshell petals snapped at fish that darted by. Crawling multilegged creatures that resembled helmeted pill bugs squirmed through the ooze, cracking and devouring snails as large as pumpkins. Sponges like rubbery tubes sucked in warm water, filtering out microorganisms, while ribbony sea snakes glided by.

Everything Polly saw seemed to have a lot of teeth.

A creature that looked like a cross between a crocodile and a swordfish cruised in front of them, attracted by the P-40's lights. The plane's churning propeller made the monster reconsider its attack, and it darted off with a thrash of its sharp tail, chomping on two unfortunate fish as it fled.

"How far do we have to go yet, Joe?"

"We didn't exactly have maps of this passage. I can only hope the inlet penetrates to the core of the island. We'll just have to wait and keep our eyes open."

Before long, the character of the water around them changed. Shafts of sunlight penetrated through a break in the cave ceiling, giving the widening grotto a lambent glow. Predatory fish swam into the streaming light, then dove back into the comforting shadows of the inlet passage.

"Nap time is over." Sky Captain tilted the rudder so his plane angled toward the light. "I'm taking us up."

"Nap time?" Polly gave an annoyed sigh. "Fresh air sounds fine with me."

With a rush of bubbles, the Warhawk climbed out of the underwater cove and surfaced in a lagoon half covered by floating leaves and odd frilled lily pads. Startled amphibians dove into the water and splashed toward the weedy shore. The plane leveled itself and came to rest afloat on the pool.

Sky Captain slid open the canopy, then stretched his arms as he drew a lungful of the heady, mulchy air. The scent of foliage and rotting vegetation made each breath seem thick enough to chew.

Polly wrinkled her nose. "Smells like a compost pile."

Sky Captain sat on top of the canopy, gazing into the island wilderness. Now the two had a chance to look around at the dense, nightmarish jungle. The strange noises of unseen creatures came from every direction: clacking insect buzzes, howls and grunts, eerie whistles.

The sunlight shimmered and reflected in the steamy air, as if slowed down by plowing into the past. Giant rushes and wide-spreading ferns rose around them, dripping star points of dew. Squat armored fern trees towered overhead, some rising almost a hundred feet high. Primitive evergreens and trees with no flowers clustered in the wet undergrowth.

Sky Captain tapped Polly on the shoulder, put a finger to his lips, and pointed off into the forest. She turned, then couldn't believe her eyes. Drinking from a shallow pool were three giant protobirds with ferocious sharp beaks that looked strong enough to snip an oak tree in half. The creatures resembled ostriches, but their muscular legs reached twenty feet off the ground before connecting to disproportionately smaller bodies. One of those drumsticks would have fed a family for a week.

The floating plane rocked from an underwater disturbance, and Polly held on to Sky Captain, strictly for balance. A dark sinuous shadow emerged from the grotto below. With barely a ripple, the dorsal spine of a gargantuan creature surfaced, and a small head rose from a serpentine neck. Half-chewed water weeds dangled from its jaws as it placidly looked around, snorted stinking spray, then dipped beneath the water again.

Polly reached into the cockpit and pulled out her camera. Her face was flushed, her breathing fast. With a reporter's eye, she raised the small camera, sighting through the viewing lens. So many amazing creatures from a time long before recorded history—how could she choose which ones to photograph? After hesitating, she sadly lowered the camera.

Sky Captain watched her in disbelief. "You're not going to shoot that? Dinosaurs, prehistoric birds, sea monsters. What would your editor say?"

Polly tapped the counter gauge. "I've got two shots left, Joe. Who knows what else is waiting for us out there?"

"Suit yourself . . . but be sure to save one of the exposures for a reunion shot with me, you, and Dex."

He reached into the cockpit and rummaged in a storage compartment. He withdrew a small kit containing a compass and then a long machete. "Always come prepared. Let's go have a look and see what we can find." When he glanced at the compass, though, it spun impossibly fast. "Terrific. Now Totenkopf is scrambling the Earth's magnetic field, too."

After they made their way to shore, the ground felt spongy and damp beneath their feet. Each step made a squelching sound. Polly could smell the sharp, oily scents of the weird vegetation rising from the swamp's sultry ooze.

She ducked, biting back an outcry, as a sound like a chainsaw whizzed past her head, and she gaped at a colorful dragonfly with a wingspan of two feet. The dragonfly circled them, and Sky Captain withdrew his pistol, ready to shoot it, but the overgrown insect sped deeper into the swamp.

Billowing seed ferns and cactuslike club mosses crowded the heavy forest. A large beetle scuttled sluggishly down the fallen trunk of a fern tree, picking its way across a wet mass of algae. A stubby-legged spider the size of an apple watched them from a scale tree, but did not seem interested in prey so large.

Sky Captain and Polly slogged through the dense brush for hours. He hacked right and left with his machete, cutting a path that led them deeper into the mysterious world. Despite their crunching and thrashing, the air seemed hushed and brooding. All around them small creatures made quiet greeting sounds, like a cicada's song played backward.

Nearby, Sky Captain heard a strange chirping sound, loud and insistent. His face wrinkled with concern. "Shhh. Listen." The tall grasses and ferns cut off their line of sight in all directions. The wind began to pick up, but the sky remained clear.

Polly cocked her ear. "I've never heard anything like it."

Sky Captain started cautiously forward. The sound was like a repetitive screeching whistle, a constant demand. "It doesn't sound too dangerous." He pushed through the brush, bending thorny brambles to poke his head through a gap in the matted pampas grass. Polly shouldered her way close beside him.

They stared at a bird's nest the size of a motor home. Thick boughs and splintered tree trunks formed the walls to keep two monstrous hatchlings inside. Each prehistoric chick was the size of a small bear. Their dark eyes glittered as their heads swiveled. Both creatures looked extremely hungry. The insistent cheeping took on a different tone as they saw Sky Captain and Polly. Their hard, bear-trap beaks clacked open and shut, demanding food.

Then a much more horrible screech split the air overhead, similar in tone to the chicks' cries but several octaves lower. Sky Captain looked up as an airplane-sized shadow descended toward them, sword-like talons outstretched.

"Run!" he shouted.

29

A Treacherous Bridge
One Shot Left
Two Confessions

The pair of ravenous monster chicks tilted their heads and opened sharp beaks to screech for their mother. An answering bellow sent chills through Polly's bones. The giant flying creature dive-bombed from above. She and Sky Captain headed for cover under the tall fern trees. The angry beast swooped low enough to rip the clumpy tops of the ancient trees, thrashing to break through. Sky Captain jabbed with his machete in an attempt to chop through the undergrowth so they could flee. The curved blade sliced vines across their path, and he bolted forward, letting twigs snap back against Polly. She knocked them aside, sputtering, and ran after him.

The winged terror circled around and came at them again. The monster bird tore at the forest overhead, shrieking in frustration as it tried to rip a hole in the clattering branches. A spiny feather as long as Polly's forearm spun to the ground. The prehistoric creature snapped at the protective branches a final time, then flapped off. Sky Captain and Polly stood close together in the shadows, waiting in suspense. The attacker did not come back.

"It seems to be gone," he said, "but I don't want to count on that. Let's get moving."

He continued to chop with the machete, pretending that he knew which direction they should go. He worked his way toward the center of the island, scaring hedgehog-sized beetles that scampered off into the underbrush. Polly stumbled behind him, and the brambles became tighter, denser.

With a hefty swing of the machete, Sky Captain hacked his way through a particularly dense thicket and suddenly found his feet only inches from the edge of a sheer cliff. Panting for breath, Polly came up beside him, not expecting the sudden ledge. She swayed, then caught his arm for balance.

He shaded his eyes, facing a deep canyon that sliced directly across their path. "It's a dirty trick to put *that* in our way." He scanned up and down the impossible gorge that seemed to go on forever.

"Well . . . we could go back to the plane, set off in another direction," Polly suggested. "We might have better luck."

He rubbed a twinge in his arm. "You haven't been the one swinging a machete all this way." Instead, farther down the gorge, he spotted a possibility. "Down there—do you see it?"

She swallowed hard. "I'm not sure I want to."

Sky Captain had already made up his mind; he began picking his way along the canyon rim. A dangerous-looking bridge made of old mossy planks and frayed vine ropes spanned the gorge. Up and down the narrow canyon, silvery waterfalls from jungle streams fed a turbulent river far below.

"Totenkopf must have been here a long time." Standing at the end of the bridge, Sky Captain tested the closest plank by stomping on it with the heel of his boot. The ropes shivered ominously, and the wooden slats groaned. He made a nervous grimace that Polly couldn't see, but he was all smiles when he turned to look at her. "Seems sturdy enough to me." He gestured with his hand. "Ladies first."

"So *now* you decide to be a gentleman?" She pointed across the bridge with some authority. "It's your idea. *Go.*"

"Sure." Sky Captain walked out onto the swaying bridge, one cautious footstep at a time. "No problem." He held the side ropes for support, but he could feel them ready to fray at any moment.

Polly decided that being left behind was worse than crossing the bridge. She followed close to him, looking straight ahead instead of down. The primitive bridge creaked terribly with every step. The opposite side of the gorge did not seem to grow any closer.

They finally made it to the middle of the span, where the bridge drooped and the half-rotted planks were covered with slick moss from the waterfall mist. Then they both froze as they heard the horrible, hungry screech of the giant flying creature again. The mother bird had been circling high, out of sight far above, but now it spotted them.

Polly raised her camera to snap off a shot, but found herself wobbling without holding on to the support ropes. She stopped herself again, convinced she was bound to see something even more spectacular on this island of monsters. "Damn." Besides, she didn't want to risk dropping her camera into the deep river gorge.

The monstrous bird let out another call and began its predatory dive.

Wasting no time, Sky Captain grabbed Polly's hand, practically yanking her arm out of its socket. "Come on! Run!" They bounded across the fragile, splintering planks, racing for the other side.

But the flying creature was too fast. They would never get to the end of the bridge. Sky Captain pulled

Polly, and both of them sprawled facedown on the rickety wooden slats, staring with wide eyes at the dizzying plunge below.

Sky Captain held on, then grabbed frantically for his pistol in its holster. His fingers just brushed the weapon before it dropped through a wide crack in the slats and tumbled from the bridge. The blue steel glinted as it dropped, finally splashing into the river far below.

The monster bird slashed with its talons, and Sky Captain protectively covered Polly's back. The bridge's support ropes foiled the attack, and the whole structure thrummed as the claws hit it. The shrieking monster bird flew past the bridge, its enormous wings beating the air. It banked and began to circle around, coming back for them.

After being struck by the talons, one of the ropes nearly snapped. Sky Captain scrambled to his knees, dragging Polly with him. "We've got to get to the other side!"

But Polly pulled her arm free and turned around. "Not yet!" She spied her camera dangling by its leather strap from one of the splintered planks. "Don't you make the bridge bounce, Joe Sullivan, or I'll lose my camera."

The side rope had frayed to a thread, only an instant away from snapping. Sky Captain reddened. "Just leave it!"

The monster bird flapped toward them, its curved beak open wide to snap them up as a single morsel.

He lurched back and grabbed Polly by the hand just as she snagged the camera strap. Grinning with the camera in her hand, she did not resist as Sky Captain pulled her roughly across the bridge. With their last bit of energy, they threw themselves to the solid canyon rim just as the rope snapped. The bridge rotated, dangling by only a single strand now. Dozens of loose planks spilled out, tumbling like autumn leaves into the frothing river far below.

The two sprawled on the ground, covered with mud, but they were still too exposed. Sky Captain dragged Polly into a cluttered thicket, where they huddled under the interlocking branches and vines. The giant bird swooped past them with an angry cry, foiled again.

Polly cradled the camera, smiling, while Sky Captain collapsed in an exhausted heap. He looked at her, apoplectic. "Are you insane? Have you completely lost your mind? You could have gotten us killed, and all for a stupid camera!"

"It's not stupid. This camera is very important to me. So important that—" Then, as she looked at it, Polly's blue eyes filled with tears.

Sky Captain's anger washed away. He had always found it fundamentally impossible to endure a woman crying . . . especially a woman like Polly Perkins. He heaved a sigh. "It's okay, Polly."

Her expression was totally forlorn as she looked at the camera. "No . . . it isn't. You can never understand."

"Sorry . . . really I am. I didn't mean to—"

Polly whirled, blurting out her misery. "I . . . I shot the *ground*!"

Now he was even more baffled. "What?"

She held up the camera. "When I was running from the bird! Of all the things we've seen, all the impossible creatures on this island, I shot the *ground*!" She started to cry harder now. "I wasted a picture!"

Sky Captain couldn't stop himself from breaking into a smile. He tried to hide his amusement by starting forward out of the thicket, but she noticed. "It's not funny, Joe! I have one shot left! *One shot!*"

Sky Captain didn't answer her, but continued to chuckle quietly as he forged a new path into the uncharted jungle. They still had a long way to go and plenty of work to do until they found the stronghold of Dr. Totenkopf. Sullenly, Polly trudged along after him, stumbling on roots and muttering to herself.

As he chopped through the thick jungle brush and plowed into another rough thicket, he glanced back to see if Polly was all right. She was carefully nursing her camera. "What is it with you and that stupid camera anyway?"

Polly looked at him with quiet sincerity. She didn't seem to want to answer, then finally said in a small voice, "You gave it to me."

Sky Captain felt a warm flush creep up his cheeks. At the moment it seemed very important to continue clearing their trail. With great gusto, he whacked at a particularly tough tangle of vines.

"You don't even remember, do you?" Polly asked. "You were flying for the American volunteers in Nanjing. I was covering the evacuation of Shanghai."

"I remember," Sky Captain said quietly. "Tojo Hideki in his bathrobe."

There was more silence between them as he continued to find weeds and vines to chop, even when they weren't necessarily in the way.

"Joe, just tell me the truth. I don't care either way, I swear. I just want to know. The girl in Nanjing . . . it was Franky Cook, wasn't it?"

Sky Captain stopped and turned around. His expression had a hangdog, defeated look. "Polly . . ."

"How long were you seeing her? Just tell me. It really doesn't matter to me."

Sky Captain thrust the machete into the soft ground so that he could put both of his hands on her shoulders. He leaned close and put all the sincerity he could force into his voice. "Polly, look into my eyes. I *never* fooled around on you. *Never.*"

Polly paused, then relinquished the secret she had

held for so long. "I sabotaged your plane," she said defiantly.

The statement received the reaction she'd anticipated. "Three *months*," Sky Captain blurted, furious.

Instantly, she turned on him. "I knew it! You lousy—"

He grabbed her and clapped his hand over her mouth, muffling her rant. "Shhh! Look." His eyes flashed as he became all business again. "He's here."

Polly's expression fell, and her indignant anger disappeared as swiftly as it had come. In the yellow light of afternoon sun, she saw a hazy construction in the distance, a giant stony fortress carved into the face of a volcanic mountain.

Totenkopf.

30

A Sinister Fortress
A Grand Construction Site
Totenkopf's Ark

Dusk had fallen by the time Sky Captain and Polly made their way through the primeval jungles to Totenkopf's fortress. Together, they moved through ferns and thorny scrub to reach the gate of the ominous stronghold. Sky Captain kept watching the skies for other giant prehistoric birds, but the jungle provided sufficient cover. The only large creatures they heard nearby fled crashing through the foliage.

"It must be instinct that they've learned to fear humans," Polly said, watching the scaly back of a large reptile as it lumbered away in a panic.

"Not just any humans," Sky Captain said. "Dr. Totenkopf."

The terrain leveled off closer to the looming fortress, and they picked up the pace. Polly tripped, sprawling into a shallow trench that had been scooped out of the ground. Sky Captain extended his hand for her, then froze.

Polly picked herself up and tried to regain her composure. "No, thanks. I don't need any help," she said. "Why would Totenkopf have slaves dig useless ditches out here in the middle of nowhere?"

"Not a ditch, Polly." Sky Captain continued to stare in disbelief. "It's a claw mark, gouged into the earth."

She followed his gaze to the nearby skeleton of a giant creature looming over them. Its yellowed bones were the size of logs, and curved fangs from a long skull implied how ferocious the thing must have been in life. She saw a spiked collar and enormous shackles that had chained the monster to the front gate. "It must have been some sort of guard dog."

"Well, somebody forgot to feed him." He picked his way past the slumped skeleton. "Lucky for us." He saw the dark entrance that the monster had once guarded. "Through there."

Polly stopped. "Look, there's a second chain, leading . . . over . . ." Her words faltered as she watched the heavy shackles begin to move. The chain curled around behind a mound of boulders deeper inside the entry passage. The links clanked together, and something large snorted and growled as it moved toward the two.

For just an instant, Polly and Sky Captain held their breath. "If there's a second one, it's probably hungry," Sky Captain pointed out.

They exchanged an apprehensive glance. Then Sky Captain saw a trail of steam escaping from a narrow crevice in the mountain wall, not far from the entry tunnel. "Through here. It probably leads inside, too."

Polly nodded. "And it has the advantage of being too narrow for one of those guard things." As the growls grew louder and chuffing breath came toward them, they quickly disappeared into the crevice.

They pushed forward into the blackness. Sky Captain reached into his pocket and pulled out his trusty lighter. He held up the small flame to shine light into the cramped passage.

As they crept onward, a reddish glow came from ahead. Polly put her hand on Sky Captain's shoulder.

"Do you hear that?" In the distance, deeper inside the mountain, powerful machinery thrummed and pounded faintly.

"It's coming from that chamber." The glow grew brighter, and the walls and floor vibrated from the industrial din. A ruddy haze rose from a ventilation shaft drilled through the cave floor.

"Only one way in." He kicked off the grate covering the ventilation shaft and lowered himself until he could drop below to the next level. He lifted his hands to help Polly down. "Come on, I'll catch you."

She looked at his outstretched arms, wondering just how safe she felt around this man, and then let herself drop. He swung Polly to the stone floor without holding her for a second longer than was absolutely necessary. As she straightened her clothes, Sky Captain was already edging his way to a rocky ledge that opened into a massive cavern. Polly caught up with him and stopped to stare at the incredible panorama. Once again, she wished she had more film. A lot more.

Though it was dazzlingly illuminated with harsh lightbulbs, the interior of Totenkopf's industrial fortress stretched on into vague dimness in all directions. The sloping, rocky ceiling rose at least six hundred feet above their heads.

"There it is," Sky Captain said. "I never would have believed . . ."

The center of the huge cavern was filled with a towering rocket ship under construction. The enormous cylinder rose from one stage to the next to the next, surrounded by catwalks, lift platforms, and scaffolding. The heavy rivets of the rocket's hull plating looked like tiny specks, conveying the enormity of the construction. Prominent on the side of the rocket, Totenkopf's winged skull emblem leered out at them.

"It must be at least as tall as the Empire State Building," Polly said.

"I've never seen the like. No one has."

Polly had expected to see slave workers like the hideously deformed man from the Shangri-La uranium mines. Instead, every aspect of the construction process was automated. Robots in jet packs buzzed like insects around the structure. Machines of every size and description operated heavy equipment. Hovering freight transports passed below, loading the storage chambers of the immense missile with crates, supplies, fuel.

Totenkopf had built a vast automated facility for ship construction and maintenance. Its scale and complexity staggered the imagination—a place for the manufacture of the enormous robot monsters that had terrorized Manhattan and other cities around the world, as well as the squadrons of Flying Wings and the undersea crab-walker robots.

Giant gears turned in synchronized harmony, like the precision works of a massive clock. Stamping presses turned sheet metal into specialized components. Sparks flew from armies of robotic arc welders. More and more of the mechanical titans were assembled, hour after hour, day after day, without stop.

Down on the floor of the chamber, boxcars on rails delivered row after row of caged animals. Even from so far away, Sky Captain and Polly could discern elephants, horses, camels, lions. Robots removed the animal cages from the railcars, and heavy lifting machines methodically loaded the specimens inside the rocket ship. The train looped around to pick up another load of cages.

Sky Captain's brow furrowed. "What is he doing with all those animals? Does Totenkopf want a private zoo?"

Polly studied the cages more closely. Two by two. Thousands of them. A look of realization crossed her face. "My God, Joe, it's an ark! He's building an ark."

On impulse, she raised the camera. She tried to frame the best photograph to could show the awe-inspiring complex. Everything was so huge, so breathtaking. Even with her own eyes and her imagination, she couldn't encompass it all, and it certainly wouldn't fit in a single frame. She stared through the viewfinder, but when she was about to snap the picture, she slowly lowered the camera with a sigh.

Sky Captain looked at her and then to the towering rocket in disbelief. "What are you doing?" The robot laborers continued their diligent work. Railcars delivered another load of animal breeding pairs. "You honestly think you're going to find something more important than Earth creatures being led two by two inside a giant rocket ship?"

"I just might."

"Like what?"

"I'll know it when I see it," Polly said. "After what we've been through so far, you shouldn't be so skeptical."

A harsh voice blared over a loudspeaker system in German. The words themselves sounded metallic. Sky Captain turned to Polly. "Do you understand any of what it's saying?"

A look of grim realization crossed her face. "Sounds like they've started a countdown."

They exchanged an ominous glance. "We're not a moment too soon." Then Sky Captain spied a catwalk just below their ledge. It appeared to lead deeper inside the labyrinth. "We've got to find Totenkopf. Follow me."

"All right, Joe. But we have to be quiet. We don't want any of those robots to hear us." As Polly moved behind him, her foot kicked a small rock, which dropped off the side of the ledge. It clanged loudly as it bounced off, falling for what seemed like an eternity, careening against catwalks and ductwork. The echoes continued to ring out until the loose stone hit the steel-plated floor with a final resonating *boom*.

Sky Captain looked at her, stunned. "You've got a gift. An absolute *gift*."

Polly swallowed hard and looked at him, apologetic. Her shoulders gave the briefest shrug.

Below them, all the machines stopped. Robot workers hovered in their jet packs, turning toward the distant ledge. The construction around the rocket became eerily quiet. Only the impatient trumpeting of a caged elephant broke the tense moment.

"Don't move," whispered Sky Captain. "Maybe they won't see us."

When they heard a noise from behind, the two of them spun around to see the mysterious woman they had encountered in Dr. Jennings's laboratory. The dark-clad woman stepped forward, pointing a strange weapon at them.

Sky Captain could barely react before the woman clobbered him on the chin. He was knocked sprawling backward to the ground, stunned. He gripped his ribs and muttered, "That . . . hurt."

Polly dropped next to him on the ledge, then stood indignantly to protect him. "What did you do to him? You leave him alone! You—"

The mysterious woman did not utter a word as she calmly stepped closer. She raised a small device and depressed a button. Then a brilliant flash of electrical discharge enveloped Sky Captain and Polly.

31

Treated like Garbage
A Happy Reunion
A New Utopia

When Sky Captain awoke with a groan, he found Polly next to him, her body pressed intimately close. He smiled briefly, but then he noticed that his hands were tied above his head. So were hers. Sky Captain struggled to swivel his shoulders, turning his face so that it was only inches from Polly's.

Her eyes were already wide and blinking at him. "Why does this keep happening to us, Joe?"

"At least you managed to keep your pants on this time," Sky Captain said.

"Not funny."

"Neither is the end of the world." Around them, echoing through the walls and reverberating through the floor, came the sounds of heavy machinery and hissing steam. Dr. Totenkopf's diabolical plans continued without rest.

Sky Captain recalled the cages of animals they had seen from their high vantage: male and female, two by two. He was struck with a horrible thought, but didn't dare speak it aloud, knowing what Polly would say. What if the mad genius intended the two of them to be breeding specimens as well? Sky Captain squirmed, pulling at the chains that bound his hands.

His body ached, his head pounded, and he found it difficult to focus his eyes. He wondered what kind of stun ray the mysterious woman had used. If they ever managed to rescue Dex, he would probably want one of them for his lab.

Sky Captain yanked hard, hoping to tear the iron manacles loose or to slip his hands through the clamps, but he succeeded only in scraping his wrists raw. Exhausted, he sagged.

Polly looked around her in the small chamber that held them. The metal walls continued to vibrate. "Where are we?"

"You'd think with the grand scale of everything he does, Totenkopf could have given us a larger prison cell." He kicked at the wall. "This place is barely larger than a closet!"

"Or your cockpit."

Sky Captain strained his head to catch a glimpse through a narrow opening. The walls lurched as if in a powerful, localized earthquake, swinging Polly against him.

"We're moving." He could see the tall rocket framed in the distance. They were on the floor of the vast construction room, lurching along, being taken somewhere. "This isn't a cell. It's some kind of container."

Polly stood on her tiptoes, peering through the same gap. "Maybe they're loading us onto the ship."

Pulling the chains to their maximum extent, Sky Captain managed to look through another air vent on the other side of the container. Pressing his face close, he caught his breath. "It's not the ship, Polly. No, that would be the good news."

She shouldered herself up to the view, and her face turned ashen. They were bound inside a steel-walled container that moved along a conveyer belt across the main floor of the impossible complex. Rattling elevators and moving conveyor belts wound through a maze of scaffolding and overhangs. Glowing rivers of molten metal ran in troughs, dumping material into molds. Ingots rolled past giant swinging hammers and busy robot arms.

But the extraneous material and scrap components were all headed toward one final destination: a gargantuan crushing machine. The container that held Sky Captain and Polly was on the same track.

With a rattling bump, their cage arrived at a transfer station where several tracks and conveyor belts intersected. Giant sorting machines reached out with mechanical claws to pluck the scrap metal from auxiliary conveyor belts. Controlled by a monstrous central robot head, the hydraulics whirred and pistons pumped with a gust of steam exhaust. With a flurry like a drunken spider trying to walk, articulated arms seized components, swiveled them into place, and released the hooked clamps to drop large chunks onto the main conveyor belt that fed the giant compactor.

"We're next in line," Sky Captain said.

Their cage suddenly lurched and swung as a giant metal claw rattled down on a control cable and clamped around the metal walls. Sharp points screeched against the steel, compressing to get a good grip. As the sorting arm lifted them, the controller hesitated, letting them dangle in midair instead of placing them on the main conveyor belt. With a rattle of chains, the cage was lifted even higher. Through the tiny opening in the metal cage, Sky Captain and Polly stared at the cyclopean metal visage. In a feeble display of foolish courage, Polly stuck her tongue out at it.

A small hatch opened on top of the colossal machine head, dropped with a clang, and a young man climbed out, grinning at them.

Sky Captain and Polly cried out in unison, "Dex!"

Caught up in their exhilaration, the two hugged each other.

At the sight of Sky Captain and Polly embracing, Dex let out a pleased sigh. "Great! You two made up."

Polly drew away, embarrassed and self-conscious. "Does he have to say that every time he sees us together?"

"He's just hoping." Sky Captain turned to the young man, raising his voice over the clamor of sorting machines, industrial stations, and the destructive percussion of the compactor apparatus. "We've been all across the world, Dex. Thank God we found you!"

"Yes," Polly piped up. "We're here to rescue you."

Standing atop the mammoth robot head, Dex stared down at the two of them trapped and bound inside the cage. "Rescue me, Cap? Hmm, from what I can see—"

Sky Captain cut him off. "Just get us out of here, Dex. Okay?"

"Hold on." Working levers and controls from inside the giant machine head, Dex caused the sorting arm to gently lower them to the ground; then he released the claw clamp. "Wait a second. I think this'll do it." He maneuvered another mechanical hand to grip the cage while a second set of claws tore off the top of the cage like a child removing the cap from a milk bottle.

Dex scrambled down the side of the giant sorting machine and quickly moved through the opening he'd just made in their container. He dropped beside them. "Well, here we are. Good to see you again Cap . . . and Polly."

Sky Captain rattled the chains binding him to the metal wall. "How much time is left on the countdown?"

Dex pulled out a hand instrument from the pocket of his overalls, pushed a button on the shaft, and a small spinning blade popped out the other end. "We've got about ten minutes before it hits the fan." He lifted the tool toward Sky Captain's metal cuffs. He touched the grinding blade to a chain link and was rewarded with a shower of sparks and a shrill screech.

"Dex hon, those vials Dr. Jennings gave me. Do you know what they are?" Polly swung aside, trying to give him room to work.

The young man paused in his cutting. "Adam and Eve. Totenkopf's masterpiece, cast in his own warped image. The result of his cruel experiments . . . and whatever's born from those vials will no longer be human."

The explanation still didn't make any sense to Sky Captain. "What is this whole place, Dex? What's going on?" From his experience, it was easier to foil a villain once he knew the overall plan.

Dex explained what he had learned during his captivity. "Dr. Totenkopf believed the Earth was doomed anyway, that we'd finally developed the technology to destroy ourselves. He didn't want to be around when that happened, so he proposed the unthinkable: to build a ship that would carry the building blocks of a new civilization into space."

"It is an ark," Polly said.

"But he intended to take only the best. He wanted a master race, a perfect order. He used his carefully programmed machines to collect specimens that represented all life on Earth. It would be the seeds of a technological utopia. Totenkopf called it his World of Tomorrow."

"Like the theme of the World's Fair," Polly said.

"Only a lot more sinister," Sky Captain said.

Even without Dex inside the robot controller head, the automated systems could pause only so long. The sorting arms began moving again, lifting clamps and grabbing scrap components.

"Uh-oh," Dex said, then applied his grinding wheel to the manacles. Suddenly, one of the giant sorting machines seized their battered cage. Dex stopped cutting so he could grab hold. He steadied himself just as the cage was unceremoniously dropped onto the main conveyer belt with a bone-jarring crash.

"Well, here we are again," Polly said.

Abruptly, they started moving straight toward the mouth of the gargantuan crushing machine. Compacting hammers battered all scrap into a shapeless mass. The conveyor belt seemed to pick up speed.

"Dex!" Sky Captain yelled, rattling his chains.

"I'm on it." The young man fired up his whirling blade and bent back to Sky Captain's cuffs. Sparks flew everywhere, and sweat streamed down his face.

Polly seemed to ignore their imminent messy death under the gargantuan crushers as she put thoughts and clues together in her mind. "So the few surviving Unit Eleven scientists smuggled those vials off the island. They knew Totenkopf would never leave without his precious genetic samples."

Dex looked at Polly with a dramatic nod. He lifted the whirling blade from Sky Captain's cuffs so she could hear him. "That's right. But now that he's got the test tubes back, there's nothing left to keep him here."

Sky Captain felt exasperated. This didn't sound like a particularly awful situation, as far as maniacal schemes went. "Then let Totenkopf go, and good riddance. He's free to set up shop where he can't harm anyone else."

Dex's expression of deadly concern showed that there was much more to the story, though. "Whatever happens, Cap, we can't let that ship leave this Earth. There's something else—"

The crashing blows of the compactor machine sounded louder, closer. Sky Captain suddenly grimaced, incredulous that Dex had stopped sawing. "Dex! We can talk about this later."

"Sorry, Cap." Dex went back to work, attacking Sky Captain's cuffs with a greater sense of urgency. It didn't seem possible that he would have enough time to free them both.

But Polly still wanted to know the answers. "Why? What haven't you told us, Dex?"

Sky Captain added, "But don't stop cutting while you explain!"

The young man shouted over the buzzing cutter. "The rocket's design is radical. Only Totenkopf really understands it. The engines use a powerful radioactive energy source unlike anything previously invented, though I did read about something similar in *Amazing Stories*."

Dangling on her chains, Polly brightened with a look of realization. "The uranium from the mine!"

"Atomic fuel. It releases a great deal of energy, enough to take that rocket anywhere. Unfortunately, there are certain . . . side effects."

"Why? What's going to happen, Dex?"

The young man paused again to emphasize the import of his words. "When the rocket reaches its third stage, the igniting engines will cause an unstoppable chain reaction in our atmosphere. Earth will be incinerated."

32

The End of the World
The Remnants of Unit Eleven
A Deadly Booby Trap

At the moment, though, they had more immediate problems. The conveyor belt pulled them along steadily, closer and closer to the unavoidable gauntlet of hissing hydraulic metal hammers and blades. Sky Captain struggled with his chains as Dex continued to cut.

Polly turned to the young man. Even with their imminent peril, she could not shake the image of the world as a charred ball. "The rocket's countdown is already started. How do we stop it?"

Dex shook his head. "Believe me, Polly, I wish I knew. I've racked my brains, studied the master control systems, but only Totenkopf himself can stop it now—and none of us has been allowed near him. I've never even seen the guy. He's too well guarded."

Before Dex had a chance to finish cutting, Sky Captain twisted one hand free. He flexed his fingers to get the blood flowing again. "So where is he, Dex? I'll go get him myself . . . as soon as you get me out of here."

Feeling Sky Captain's determination, Dex went to work on his other hand. "I'll bet you will, Cap!"

"Uh . . . boys?" Polly said. The massive crusher was just ten feet away.

Sky Captain yanked his arm, but a chain still bound his other wrist. Polly struggled, unable to move. Dex spun the grinder, furrowing his brow as if he contemplated how he might make it more efficient, but there was simply no way he could free them from their bonds in time.

The young man looked up, helpless. "Um, Cap? Do you want me to stay here to the end?" It didn't seem polite to cut Sky Captain loose and leave Polly dangling there to be pulverized in the crusher.

The smashers came down with the sound of colliding cement trucks. The conveyor belt drew their cage into the yawning mouth of the compacting machine.

"Joe? I—" Polly called.

Then the conveyor belt ground to a halt. The rollers creaked, fountains of steam hissed out of hot machinery, and the massive hammers froze in midstrike. In a breathless moment, the cage that held Sky Captain, Polly, and Dex teetered at the precipice of the crusher's mouth.

Polly looked up through the torn-away roof of their cage to see three old men standing over them on a walkway. One of the men yanked harder on the lever that had stopped the conveyor belt, locking it into place. The old men all wore stained and patched lab smocks, and their wispy white hair had not been cut in some time. They waved.

Smiling, Dex returned the greeting. "Cap, Polly, I'd like you to meet the talented gentlemen who built this place. They're the only ones left."

A look of realization crossed Polly's face. The men were decades older now, and the intervening years had obviously been hard on them, but she recognized their faces from the old photograph: Dr. Kessler, Dr. Lang, and Dr. Vargas.

"Unit Eleven," she said.

*   *   *

Minutes later, after Sky Captain and Polly were both freed from their chains, they ran with Dex and the three old scientists down a rocky passageway. They knew they didn't have much time until the end of the countdown.

Ahead of them, a large arching doorway opened into a massive gallery that resembled a museum of sorts filled with all manner of natural and scientific artifacts, robotic designs, and specimen tanks.

"Looks like Totenkopf has spent a lot of time collecting trinkets," Polly said.

"And experimenting," Dr. Vargas said, "and torturing others—all in the name of science."

The centerpiece of the enormous room was the towering skeleton of a brontosaurus, much like the creature Polly and Sky Captain had seen emerging from the marshy island lake. The striking aspect of this dinosaur, though, was that it had two heads and two long and sinuous necks branching from its trunk. Polly and Sky Captain exchanged an amazed look, but they had too little time to stand staring at a freak show.

The three Unit Eleven scientists briskly led them to the far end of the gallery. Obviously frightened, they crept against the wall until they rounded a diorama display case. Dr. Vargas took Polly's wrist to get her attention and pointed to the entrance of a primary laboratory. Huge iron doors sported the winged-skull emblem of their nemesis.

Two menacing robots twice the height of a man guarded the forbidding doorway. Next to the machine sentinels, conical and exotic transformers rose like sculptures, resembling giant Tesla coils on either side of the doorway.

"Through there," Dex said. "Totenkopf's inside, hiding and protected. That's the only way in."

"No matter how hard we might try, there is no way past them," Dr. Vargas said.

Throughout the cavernous industrial facility, loud-speakers continued to boom out the countdown in German. Polly turned to Sky Captain, anxious. "Only five minutes left, Joe."

Sky Captain surveyed the area briefly, then turned to the group beside him. "Wait here." He cracked his knuckles, then rounded the corner of the display case. "Sometimes you have to meet a problem head-on."

"I don't think his *head*'s got anything to do with this," Polly muttered.

Dr. Vargas called after him. "What are you doing, man? You'll be killed!"

Sky Captain strode boldly ahead, and the long-dormant sentinel machines suddenly came to life. Heavy gears clicked and whirred as they straightened, swiveled, and turned their blazing optical sensors toward the intruder. In unison, the sentinel robots took two plodding steps to block his way.

Facing them like a gunfighter in the Old West, Sky Captain reached inside his flight jacket and produced Dex's new Buck Rogers ray gun. He pointed the noz-zle, sighted along the guide fin, and pushed the red firing button. Shimmering rays blasted the first ma-chine's body core, melting a hole through the armored torso. The robot slumped in half, its jointed legs fold-ing outward like a chicken's; then it slumped to the floor.

Undaunted, the second sentinel robot lurched toward Sky Captain, who swiveled his body and pointed the nozzle, but the futuristic gun failed to work. The metal sentinel plodded closer, stretching out powerful arms that ended in clamping claws.

"Dex? I'd appreciate any advice you might have." Sky Captain sounded cool, but his voice cracked a little.

Dex peeked out from behind the display. "Try shak-ing it. Sometimes that works."

Sky Captain scuttled backward to stay away from

the looming sentinel robot. He rattled the gun in his hand, raised it, and pushed the red button repeatedly, but only a small burst sputtered out. The beam did melt a hole in part of the robot's spindly leg shaft, and it wobbled slightly. Seeing the machine's momentary unbalance, Sky Captain lunged for it, throwing all his weight until he succeeded in pushing the sentinel over. Like a turtle on its back, the heavy overturned robot writhed and kicked.

The loudspeaker overhead continued the droning countdown. Another minute had elapsed.

Now that the guardians had been removed from the sealed door to Totenkopf's inner sanctum, Dr. Kessler jumped to his feet. "Quickly! We must hurry. Listen to the time!" Spry for an old man, he bounded between the massive transformers that stood on either side of the sealed door.

Sky Captain sensed something at the last moment and shouted, "Doctor, stop!"

Kessler stepped on a metal floor plate between the transformers, and the rings and wires instantly crackled to life. Giant forks of electricity lashed out, pinning the old scientist like an insect in amber. Static and sparks tore through his body. For a mercifully brief instant, he screamed as he was consumed in flames. Through sheer momentum, his blackened skeleton staggered one step farther before it fell to the ground in pieces.

Lightning continued to arc back and forth between the paired transformers, weaving a web of electricity that seemed alive with dazzling bluish currents. Shadows and a more solid shape began to congeal inside the dense electrical field: a giant holographic image of a man's sunken, gaunt, and impassioned face. The projection sharpened to crystal clarity, a visage sure to cause nightmares.

Trembling, Vargas looked up at the giant display. "That's him. Dr. Totenkopf."

33

The Face of Totenkopf
An Inner Sanctum
The Ghost of a Genius

The shimmering hologram looked down on them, its shadowy eyes cavernous. The mouth opened and closed, uttering German words in a thunderous, menacing voice: *"Was begonnen wurde kahn nicht gehaltet werden. Verlasse den Platz oder sterbe. Sie sind gewarnen."*

Polly turned to Dr. Vargas. "I can't understand it all. What exactly is he—"

The old scientist translated. "He says, 'What has begun cannot be stopped. Leave this place or die. You are warned.' Totenkopf always talked like that, even when it wasn't about anything important."

"Yeah, the usual warnings." Sky Captain looked at the shimmering, ominous projection and frowned. He turned to Polly. "Did you see that new movie *The Wizard of Oz*?"

"Not all of it."

The booming ultimatum began to repeat, when the hologram suddenly fizzled away. The twinned transformers sparked, hummed, and died.

Dex stood by the insulated base of the nearest transformer, holding a tangle of wires he had yanked from the control panel like a gardener uprooting particularly noxious weeds. "I think we've heard enough of his babbling. That disables the whole defensive system."

Knowing how little time remained, a determined Sky Captain marched toward the transformers. He took one step, hesitating at the point where Dr. Kessler had been incinerated. "You sure it doesn't have any juice left, Dex?"

The young man shrugged. "There's only one way to find out. You want me to—"

"No, Dex. It'll be us." With a grim but confident expression, Polly reached out and seized Sky Captain's hand. She pulled him with her, and the two of them stepped over the threshold between the transformers. Both of them showed relief on their faces as they emerged safely on the other side.

They turned back to Dex, who looked at them, flabbergasted. "Shazam! I meant test it by *throwing something*."

Sky Captain shrugged sheepishly. "Well, our way worked. Come on, we've got a mad genius to visit."

The two Unit Eleven scientists moved past Dex as he left the tangle of wires on the disabled transformer. All five of them passed through the ominous iron doors and into Totenkopf's study.

The inner sanctum of the mad scientist was not quite what they were expecting. The study was a quaint reading room, cozy and well-appointed, with leather-bound books neatly arranged on shelves. Everything had been put into perfect order, but the air had a sour staleness, as if they were the first people to move there in decades. On a corner table, cut-crystal glasses sat next to an empty sherry decanter.

A mahogany desk was piled with yellowed papers and age-cracked lab notebooks. Dex and the two old scientists huddled around Totenkopf's desk, sorting through documents covered with dust.

But they saw no sign of the mastermind. "He's not here," Polly said. "We're too late."

Dr. Vargas blew dust off a ledger sheet. "These are his personal papers. Totenkopf would never leave without them." He tapped the crumbling book. "He must still be here."

Dr. Lang sneezed from the dust, then blinked red-eyed at all the notes and journals. "Only that man can stop this terrible tragedy from occurring. We must find him."

While the others concentrated on the desk, Sky Captain ventured deeper into the room and found an alcove filled with elaborate control panels, a communication screen, and a transmitter.

"I found him," he called, but his voice carried no jubilation. "But Totenkopf isn't in any condition to stop a thing."

In front of the elaborate control panel, the dark outline of a figure sat in a high-backed leather chair. The others looked up as Sky Captain flicked on a lamp. Bright yellow light flooded down on the face of Dr. Totenkopf.

Unlike the grim and threatening visage that had been projected on the shimmering transformer field, the real evil genius was shriveled and mummified. Totenkopf had died at his controls, and his desiccated remains lay back in the seat, slumped in rotted repose.

Polly hurried over, stunned. "It can't be. It's impossible!"

Dex came up behind the chair, unable to believe what they were seeing. "But all those robots," Dex said. "The rocket ship, the plan to destroy Earth—it's happening right *now*, in 1939, but he looks like he's been dead for a very long time." He sniffed the musty, tainted stench that clung to the body. "Smells like it, too."

Under the bright light of the lamp, Sky Captain noticed a slip of paper in Totenkopf's shriveled hand.

He reached down and pried the paper from the mummy's grip. He unrolled the brittle scroll and found two words scribbled in German. He showed them to Dr. Vargas, who read them aloud, " 'Forgive me.' "

Sky Captain let out an angry snort. "We won't have much chance to do that, unless we can stop the disaster in the next few minutes."

From a table beside the control banks, Dex picked up a large, leather-bound notebook and began to flip through the age-browned pages. "His journal." He squinted down to decipher the shaky handwriting. "The last entry was made on October 11, 1918." He looked up, stunned. "He died more than twenty years ago."

Sky Captain wadded the crumbling apology letter and dropped the dusty fragments to the floor. "We've been chasing a ghost to the four corners of the Earth."

Polly touched his shoulders. "Those giant robots in Manhattan weren't ghosts, Joe. Or the Flying Wings that wiped out the Legion's base, or that mysterious woman who killed Dr. Jennings and knocked us both unconscious."

Dex found himself intrigued by the control panels. He smeared dust from glass gauges and engraved plates that identified systems. With complete confidence, or just reckless curiosity, he started flipping switches. Indicator lamps illuminated, a sparkling sequence of red, yellow, and green.

"Blinking lights," Dex said. "That's a good sign."

Without thinking, he almost sat down in the high-backed chair, but stopped himself before he could drop into the mummy's lap. One switch seemed more prominent than the others, so Dex flipped it without hesitating because they didn't have time for caution.

The low bass hum of large machinery increased. The thick metal shutters forming one wall of the mad genius's inner sanctum began to grind aside to reveal a broad picture window. Totenkopf's empire of enslaved machines lay revealed before them.

Breathing quickly, they gathered at the window to watch as hundreds upon hundreds of robots toiled endlessly in the background. The entire island had been transformed into a single organism that was dedicated to one task.

"Totenkopf had his great plan, and he programmed all his robots with very precise instructions," Dex said. "Even after he died, they never stopped, his machines. Those worker robots are finishing what they were programmed to do. They don't need their master anymore to complete their task."

Dr. Vargas placed his hands flat against the glass of the broad window. "Don't you see? This entire island is Totenkopf. Every wire, every gear. He's found a way to cheat even his own death."

"So how do you kill someone who's already dead?" Polly asked. "And by the way, we've only got a minute or two left to do it."

Suddenly, a low rumble throbbed through the giant complex. The entire mountain began to shake. The two surviving Unit Eleven scientists looked at each other.

The rumble became louder and louder, and the floor was jolted by the force of immense rocket engines igniting. Totenkopf's desiccated cadaver swiveled in the chair.

Sky Captain turned to Dex. "How do we stop it?"

Old Dr. Vargas shook his head and turned away from the window. "Nothing can stop the end of the world now."

34

A Deadly Countdown
A Painful Good-bye
A Final Face-Off

As vented rocket exhaust roared out of the wide cones at the base of the gantry structure, Totenkopf's control room itself started to collapse. The ceiling buckled, and a long crack split the glass of the viewing window. Debris rained down from the quaking force of the rocket ship's engines.

Polly ducked, shielding her head. "There must be a way to cut it off!"

Dr. Vargas and Dr. Lang huddled together, chattering in heated German, tossing desperate ideas back and forth, and then dismissing every one. Dex looked at the two old men, hoping to contribute. Totenkopf's notes and journals lay strewn across the desk, but it was far too much information to absorb in a few seconds.

Figuring that he couldn't possibly make matters worse, Dex furiously worked the control panel, slapping switches and cutting off power systems. As the rocket's thrust continued to build, automated systems across the entire complex shorted out. Dex reeled backward, covering his face from a fountain of sparks. Smoke curled from the control panel. "I don't think I pushed the right button."

Scratching his goatee, Dr. Vargas turned back to Sky Captain. He wore a hangdog expression. "Even if it were possible, Totenkopf's machine defenders would never allow us to get close enough to succeed. They won't permit anything to interfere with their programming."

Sky Captain squared his shoulders. "You let me worry about the damned machines." He cracked his knuckles. "Just show me what to do."

"May as well let him try," Dr. Lang said.

Vargas led Sky Captain to the dusty mahogany desk and unrolled the schematics to the rocket ship. "We worked on this design. The scientists of Unit Eleven were familiar with its capabilities. It was our job to determine—and eliminate—any flaws or weaknesses. But on such a monumental construction, it is not possible to achieve perfection." He lowered his sad eyes. "Some of us did not want to."

With a yellowed fingernail, he pointed out an electrical conduit that ran through the rocket's control module. "Here, observe closely."

Dr. Lang joined him, so excited he could speak only in German. Vargas replied, and both of them explained in rapid-fire words. Sky Captain looked at the two old men, lost.

Dex stepped in. "They say if you can cut the lead in the system terminal, it should create a short that will ignite the fuel line before the rocket can reach its third stage." He grinned. "Big explosion. No more rocket, no more problem, no more end of the world."

Sky Captain felt relieved but puzzled by the plan's simplicity. "That's it? That's all I have to do?" He slapped Dex on the back. "Let's go, then. No time to waste. Where's this—"

"The terminal is on board the rocket, Cap." The young man's face was grave. "And . . . once you cut the lead, there won't be time for you to escape."

Sky Captain froze, then came to terms with the situation. "Well, there's no use crying about it. We're talking about saving the world." He took a long breath, then turned solemnly to Polly. "Get Dex and the scientists to safety. You know where my Warhawk is. Dex can fly her . . . probably." The young man blushed. "Contact Franky as soon as you're off the island. She'll know what to do from there."

Polly put her hands on her hips. "What are you talking about, Joe? I'm coming with you."

"Not this time."

"We had a deal! You're not leaving without me— not when things are finally getting interesting." Polly held up her camera, insistent. "Besides, I still have to take my last photo." She didn't want to think that the final picture on the roll of film would show the rocket exploding, with Sky Captain on board. Then Polly surprised both of them by giving him an emotional embrace. "I won't let you—"

A calm suddenly came over him as he gazed into her blue eyes. His voice softened. "I wish we had more time, Polly. I only hope you can forgive me someday."

Polly looked at him quizzically. "Forgive you? Oh, for Nanjing . . . ?"

"No. For this." Sky Captain pulled Polly close, kissing her hard. Then, without warning, he swung back and punched her squarely in the jaw. Knocked unconscious, Polly collapsed into Dex's waiting arms. The young man caught her, looking surprised.

"Take care of her, Dex."

"Sure, Cap." He struggled to hold on to Polly's limp form as Sky Captain raced out of the room. "Good luck."

The rocket's engines built up thrust for takeoff, consuming more and more fuel. The skyscraper-tall structure strained against the clamps holding it in place until the output had reached its maximum levels.

Setting his flight goggles over his eyes so he could see through the caustic fumes and stinging smoke, Sky Captain fought his way through the growing inferno as the island continued to shake. The intense vibrations made him reel from side to side. He ducked from an erratically swinging robot arm connected to an assembly line, then careened into a burly mechanical worker, then tripped and sprawled to the ground.

Robotic janitors followed their programming, striving in vain to keep the work floor tidy.

Sky Captain hauled himself to his feet and continued to fight his way through the rocky chamber. The chaos grew worse the closer he got to the rocket ship, but he staggered forward.

He finally emerged on the launch bay, where he skidded to a stop. The mysterious black-clad woman stood there facing him, her arms at her sides. She adjusted her opaque goggles and turned a stony, perfect face toward him. She looked as if she had been waiting for him all along.

Sky Captain sighed, already exhausted by the thought of facing her again. But this woman was the only thing standing between him and the rocket.

They slowly circled each other, squaring off. He balled his fists. "All right. How do you want to do this?"

She swung her fist so fast he barely saw the blur. With a single blow, the woman knocked Sky Captain flat on the ground.

Dex and Dr. Vargas both carried Polly's unconscious body, while Dr. Lang led the way. "Here! Through this storage area!"

"We have to get away, Fritz!" Vargas cried, struggling to hold on to Polly's feet. Another chunk of the ceiling fell, crashing onto Totenkopf's neat desk.

"I know, I know!" Dr. Lang opened a sealed door

at the rear of the inner sanctum. He argued rapidly in German, insisting that they hurry.

Out of breath, Dex followed. "With all these huge machines around here, isn't there *one* that could help us escape?"

"Of course," Vargas said. "Where do you think we are going?"

When they made their way into the echoing storage area, Dr. Lang raced toward a giant transport machine. "*Ach!* Here we are!" He yanked a grease-spotted tarpaulin off the front of a massive hovercraft cargo hauler.

"It's beautiful," Dex said, admiring the design. "And right now that craft is just what we need."

Lang moved boxes aside, tossing useless packages overboard in order to clear a space on the floor. Dex and Dr. Vargas laid Polly gently on the deck of the hovercraft, resting her head on a rolled blanket. After making sure she was safe, Dex scrambled toward the front section and its control panels. "I'm sure I can figure this thing out . . . fast enough, I hope."

Tucked on the floor of the craft, Polly fluttered her eyes, slowly regaining consciousness.

Dex scanned the controls and gauges, figuring them out in a flash. The large red button was an obvious place to start. He depressed it, and the lower engines roared to life as fans spun, compressing air and providing lift. As soon as they cleared the ground, he pulled back on a control stick. The transport heaved itself forward.

With a vibrating whistle of air, the lumbering transport moved slowly out of the collapsing cavern. Fragments of falling rock pummeled the sides of the hovercraft. The vehicle picked up speed, rushing toward the cavern's exit.

Dr. Lang stood beside Dex at the controls. "We used to fly this hovercraft all around the island. The best views of the volcano! But we had to stop when the prehistoric birds began to attack us. Poor Dr. Schmidt . . ."

Vargas clung to a railing on the opposite side of Dex. "Perhaps I should just have remained aboard the *Hindenburg III*." Then the old scientist glanced back to where Polly had been resting just a moment earlier. His rheumy eyes went wide with surprise. He tapped Dex's arm. "Excuse me."

Polly was no longer aboard.

After the inhuman blow from the mysterious woman, Sky Captain skidded against a wall. He shook his head clear as he struggled to pull himself up. "All right, so you know how to show off."

He lunged at her and swung his fist in a punch that should have knocked the wind out of a dinosaur, but once again the woman was too quick and too strong. With a swirl of her dark clothes, she struck him a second time, and Sky Captain was thrown to the ground again.

He launched himself back at her, hoping to land at least one solid punch before she flattened him a third time. He did succeed in dodging an uppercut, and they struggled back and forth. But Sky Captain was pounded yet again, and he dropped to the ground with crushing force, unable to stand.

This was humiliating. He was thankful, at least, that no one else was there to see him.

By the time the silent, implacable woman stood over him, he had mustered only enough stamina to get himself to one elbow. The woman withdrew her strange electrical device and raised its emitter. He knew that if she stunned him, he would not wake up before the rocket launched.

His female foe placed a black-gloved finger over the stunner's firing button. Before she could depress it, though, something smashed across her mannequin-perfect face with a brutal clang. The woman reeled backward, dropping her electrical stun weapon.

Sky Captain blinked blood and sweat out of his eyes to see an angry-looking Polly holding a length of pipe. A nice shiner had already started to form under her eye.

Before either of them could say anything, they heard a strange clattering from where the mysterious woman was lying on the ground. Impossible. The blow from the pipe should have killed her, or at least knocked her unconscious for a week.

The two watched in disbelief as sparks shot from the woman's writhing body. Her arms and legs jittered in impossible spasms. Her round black goggles had split apart, and her faceplate had been torn away. Beneath her shattered features, they saw a complex nest of gears and wires. The murderous woman was herself a machine, probably the most sophisticated one Totenkopf had ever built.

Reeling and weak, Sky Captain slowly climbed to his feet. He swayed to catch his balance as Polly walked up to him. He wiped blood from the corner of his mouth. "What took you so long?" He had no time to duck as Polly struck him in the chin with a right cross.

"Let's go," she said, turning away from him and marching purposefully into the launch bay. "But don't think that means we're even."

Sky Captain massaged his aching chin as he staggered to his feet again. "Jeez, Polly, it was for your own good. I was trying to protect you."

Muttering, he hurried after her into the grotto at the center of the mountain base. He remembered the blueprints Dr. Vargas had showed him, forgot his annoyance with Polly (temporarily), and sprinted toward a control panel. "We've got to get out there."

The thrumming, smoking rocket seemed very far away, out in the center of the cavern.

Showing more confidence than he felt, Sky Captain flipped a series of switches, then smiled as a telescoping gantry begin to hum and extend. "There we go, door-to-door service." He worked the buttons and dials, watching the gantry as it rose up and out and approached the rocket's upper module.

As he locked the controls so the gantry would keep moving toward the rocket, Polly started to run down the narrow walkway. Neither of them could wait until it was safe. Sky Captain hurried after her, catching Polly's arm just in time as the gantry rocked unsteadily. The mountain continued to convulse and disintegrate. Heavy pieces of debris pelted the metal walkway. Chunks of rock and dislodged piping spiraled through the air, tumbling all the way to the floor, where they crushed hapless robot workers.

Jagged boulders fell from cracks in the walls, and a rough section of debris crashed into the gantry's driving machinery, jamming the huge gears. As Sky Captain and Polly scrambled to the end of the telescoping gantry, the extended metal arm lurched and came to a grinding stop.

Polly teetered on the edge of the walkway. It was a dead end, with a twenty-foot chasm still separating them from the rocket entrance. "Joe!"

With a determined sigh, Sky Captain moved Polly aside, then stepped back. "I spend most of my time flying. Now it's time to try it without the airplane."

He made a running leap, using the end of the unstable gantry as a springboard. He sailed through the air but landed just short of the rocket opening, colliding with the smooth hull. He scrabbled for a grip, pushing his sweaty palms against the metal, but he slid down. One hand just barely grasped the bottom lip of the entrance. He hung there, his feet kicking and trying to gain a toehold.

Twenty feet away, Polly could only watch as Sky

Captain struggled to pull himself up. She had no way to help him.

The roaring rocket engines shook the cavern as if the whole world was about to fall to pieces around them. Unexpectedly, one of the violent tremors knocked loose the debris that jammed the gantry's gears. The clockwork mechanism clanked and spun, and the structure began to extend forward again, closing the distance.

With brute strength and determination, Sky Captain pulled himself up, getting his other hand on the rim of the hatch. He strained, used any bit of friction from the soles of his boots, then caught the edge of a large rivet, until he got his chin over the lip of the rocket's door. A final Herculean effort let him sprawl through the doorway, swinging his legs inside. He lay exhausted and panting on the deck just as the gantry came to a soft stop at the edge of the door.

Polly stepped gracefully through the entrance and into the control module. Sweating and ready to collapse, Sky Captain looked up at her as she strolled effortlessly past him into the rocket.

"Don't just lie there, Joe. We don't have much time."

Outside, the booming loudspeaker counted down the remaining seconds until the actual launch . . . *"Fünf . . . vier . . . drei . . . zwei . . . eins—zündung !"*

Sky Captain got to his knees, lurching toward the open hatch. He swung the metal door shut and sealed the lock just as the towering ship began to lift into the air with all the noise of a thousand thunderstorms.

35

A Rocket in Flight
Emergency Systems
The End of the Plan

Accelerating fully now, Dex's hovercraft shot from the mouth of the cave fortress and cruised over the jungle. Behind them, the huge industrial complex smoked and trembled.

"Totenkopf didn't worry much about what would happen once he blasted off, did he?" Dex looked anxiously over his shoulder.

"Why should he?" Vargas said. "He meant to turn Earth into a charred ball."

"And us with it," Lang said, even paler than usual. "For decades, I have regretted ever working for Unit Eleven."

Then, with an angry screech that could have shattered crystal, a prehistoric bird came swooping toward them, as if they were to blame for all the mayhem. Its talons extended to snatch a morsel of fresh human meat from the hovercraft.

"Another one of those flying creatures! We are doomed!" Lang tried to find a place to hide under the seat. The bird's wingspan was broader than that of Sky Captain's Warhawk.

Dex struggled with the transport vehicle's controls,

but the hovercraft had not been designed to offer much maneuverability or speed.

Before the winged monster could attack, though, a tremendous explosive blast came from the heart of the secret fortress. The roar built higher as the nose of the rocket ship lifted above the thick jungle canopy.

The boom of the launch was deafening, accompanied seconds later by a hurricane-force shock wave. Startled and confused, the prehistoric bird flapped away, seeking shelter and leaving them alone.

"Shazam, that rocket's heading up! Time to get out of here," Dex yelled over the continuing rumble. The rocket ship climbed higher, tracing a fiery contrail across the blue sky.

"It's no use now!" Dr. Lang wailed. "Once the third stage ignites, the Earth will be a radioactive cinder."

"If Sky Captain made it on board, this isn't over yet." Dex sounded completely convinced. "Give him a chance."

The tremors and continuing detonations stirred the primeval forests that covered the island. Dex looked down, seeing huge dinosaurs stampeding for the coast.

Focusing on the hovercraft's control panel, he began to adjust the frequency of the radio transmitter. "Come in Manta Station. Do you read me? Come in Manta Station. Franky, it's Dex. Do you read me?"

The rocket's liftoff knocked Sky Captain and Polly to the deck, but Sky Captain climbed to his feet and staggered to a narrow metal ladder that led to the control module above. He propped himself up by hanging on to a metal rung. Every cell in his body ached, and he honestly couldn't remember ever feeling worse. Maybe if he saved the world, he'd feel better about the whole situation.

Polly followed him, stumbling. The engines were powerful enough to lift the rocket's incredible tonnage free of Earth's gravity; the acceleration certainly made it hard for her to move. But Sky Captain had already ascended ahead of her, and she wouldn't let him get too far without her.

Polly managed to climb to a series of observation portals that allowed views inside the gargantuan cargo section. Exhausted, she hung on to the rungs and paused to peer through one of the small windows. Inside the cargo section she could see the massive zoo that Totenkopf had collected: cage after cage of breeding specimens, thousands of helpless creatures trapped inside and forced to fly off into the unknown because of a dead madman's dream of creating a new Eden.

Sky Captain looked down as she stared at the trapped animals. The rocket continued to accelerate. "Polly, hurry."

She caught up just after he climbed into the primary command deck. He gave her a hand, pulling her through the hatch in the floor, and they stood together inside the huge domed chamber.

Totenkopf had left a swarm of special robots to run the operations. Hovering machines worked like insects inside a massive hive, tending controls and receiving updates and complex binary readouts. The rocket ship tore like an arrow through the atmosphere.

A gargantuan screen spanned three stories, showing layers of clouds that streaked past. At the base of the screen stood a lone, poignantly empty command chair. Totenkopf's throne, his view into the galaxy. Though he'd been dead for decades, the robots proceeded without him.

Sky Captain and Polly stepped to the edge of the deck, which dropped down onto a dizzying spectacle. Below them, the cargo hold of the ark ship trailed off into seeming infinity, circular rings of cages and tanks that held thousands of species of birds, mammals, reptiles, insects, and fish.

Polly's heart wrenched in sympathy. "We have to get those animals off this ship before the third stage explodes."

"I'd prefer to get *us* off the ship too . . . and prevent the Earth from being incinerated while we're at it."

A harsh mechanical voice clacked out of a booming loudspeaker, making an announcement in German. Polly turned to him. "Joe, there's only one minute until primary ignition."

Sky Captain stared down into the core, which dropped two thousand feet below them. Then he glanced across to see a narrow catwalk directly in front of them; it bridged the open core of the rocket and led straight to the system terminal.

"That's our only way across." He set off across the narrow gangplank. The rocket shook violently as it accelerated, continuing its rough climb. Sky Captain fought to maintain his balance. Below, the core stretched downward on such a dizzying scale he could not see the bottom of the ship. "No time for a fear of heights."

As Polly was about to follow, she noticed a nearby control panel and frowned. Hazard markings highlighted a hinged metal box on which was printed the bold word *DRINGLICHKEITSFREIGABE*.

"Emergency release," she said. Turning away from Sky Captain and his precarious balancing act, Polly lifted the steel flap on the box to find a single red button. "I think this counts as an emergency." She pushed the button.

A ratcheting alarm shrilled through the loudspeaker system. The synthesized robotic voice announced in German, "Danger. Core separation engaged."

Polly looked up, startled. "I hope that's what we wanted to do." The rocket shuddered.

On the catwalk, Sky Captain swayed back and forth with one leg uplifted. When he'd regained his balance after a breathless moment, he turned back to see Polly standing meekly at the control panel. "What did you do?" .

"Just trying to help." Guilty and cooperative now, she retreated from the control box and joined Sky Captain on the catwalk. She glanced down, fighting vertigo, and suddenly loud, hydraulic noises rumbled from below. A gargantuan metal iris closed the cargo section, sealing off the control module from the ark chambers.

"Danger," the mechanical voice repeated. "Core separation engaged."

A look of realization crossed Sky Captain's face. He turned to Polly. "Run! We've got to get to the other side!"

They tore off across the narrow steel bridge, not looking down into the open core of the ship. The rocket was shaking so violently that they could barely stand. When he was halfway across the catwalk, massive hinged latches that supported the cargo section suddenly sprang open like a crocodile's jaw releasing its prey.

"Danger. Core separation engaged."

Sky Captain grabbed Polly and held her tight as they stood suspended over the drop-off. The sound of heavy iron support girders creaked under the strain. Magenta lights flashed in warning. "Hold on!"

The center core explosively separated from the main body, throwing Polly and Sky Captain to the narrow catwalk. They sprawled on the latticework bridge and fought to hang on as the cargo section fell away. Empty air roared through the gaping hole where the iris floor had been. They could see the Earth speeding away from them: the vast ocean, the small patch of Totenkopf's island, even the curvature of the horizon.

Once jettisoned, the cargo section tumbled gracefully. Several seconds later, giant chutes deployed to catch the thousands of animal specimens and bring them to a safe landing.

Without the added weight of the lost section, the rocket suddenly and dramatically accelerated. The sounds around them were deafening. "We're picking up speed!" Sky Captain shouted.

Polly felt nauseated by the frightening drop below. "I wouldn't want to fall now. . . ."

"I didn't want to fall *before*."

"Thirty seconds to primary ignition," said the voice on the loudspeaker.

Sky Captain and Polly looked aghast. Their time had been cut in half. They crawled across the catwalk, pinned in place by the incredible acceleration.

He caught her again as the rocket began to shake violently. The thick girders that supported the interior of the control modules bent under the strain; one sheared in half, showing bright metal. "Come on, only a little farther."

They both struggled to their feet. Giant arcs of pent-up static electricity burst across their path, leaping from one contact point to another. Falling debris blocked their way. The hovering monitor robots swirled around like leaves in a tornado, smashing into each other, colliding with the curved walls. Three of them were sucked through the bottomless hole of the floor far below.

"Twenty seconds to primary ignition."

With the groan of a mortally wounded animal, one of the metal crossbeams supporting the domed roof burst free of its anchor. Rivets shot out like bullets, ricocheting against the hull. Sky Captain ducked as one whizzed past him. Dragged down by the shuddering acceleration, the huge metal girder swung down toward them, smashing into the catwalk just behind Polly's legs. The impact was like the blow of an executioner's ax; it sliced the metal bridge in half. The catwalk began to collapse.

Trying to run faster than the falling bridge, Sky Captain pulled Polly along to the edge of the control deck. They both leaped to safety just as the catwalk buckled, twisted, then detached. It swirled as it tumbled away through the open floor, hurtling toward the Earth in a violent flash.

"Ten seconds to primary ignition."

As Sky Captain and Polly got to their feet again, another concussive force knocked them to the metal deck. But they kept inching toward the system terminal with only seconds to spare. Reaching up toward the bank of lights and toggles, Sky Captain hoped he could remember the right sequence from the rocket ship's design specifications.

Then one of the hovering monitor robots swung close to him, darting toward his head. Sparks of blue electricity zapped at him, defensive measures meant to keep anyone from tampering with the systems. Sky Captain ducked as the static bolt hit him. The floater robot was like an angry hornet defending its hive.

Polly locked both of her hands together in a double fist and swung at the hovering machine. She smacked it like Babe Ruth hitting a home run. The metal robot spun out of control, bounced against the nearest wall, then dropped. As it struggled to reset its levitating engines, the machine tumbled into the roaring updraft and then fell out of the bottom of the rocket.

Polly looked at her smarting, bloodied knuckles. "I think I broke my hand!"

Sky Captain reached the controls and threw a switch. Nearby, a section of the floor panel recessed and then slid open to expose the underwiring connected to the main system station. There, protected and suspended in a glass container, hung the two vials of Dr. Totenkopf's genetic experiments.

Knowing he had done the first step correctly, Sky Captain darted his gaze back and forth across the control panel. From the emergency tool pouch inside his pilot's jacket, he withdrew a pair of small wire clippers. He had enough training and experience to do fast, necessary repairs on any plane in the Flying Legion.

This time, though, he wasn't trying to fix anything. He steadied his hand, placing the clipper blades over a single wire. He looked at Polly. They shared a silent moment, knowing they would not survive this act of heroism.

Finally, she said, "You can't wait, Joe. We have to do this—"

"I missed you, too."

Polly swallowed hard, choked with emotion. She nodded. He fit the clipper blades around the primary wire and started to squeeze.

With a darting blur, another hand seized Sky Captain's wrist, preventing him from cutting the wire. Startled, he and Polly both whirled to see the hideously exposed metal-and-circuitry face of the mysterious android woman. Her black garments were torn and melted away, leaving her synthetic body partly exposed. Bits of machinery showed through the peeling plastic flesh.

Sky Captain let out an angry groan. "Why won't you die?"

Wrenching his wrist free, he reeled back and swung, driving the pointed wire clippers into her broken faceplate. Sparks sprayed from her face like a shower of electrical blood, and her robot muscles stuttered and jittered, throwing her into convulsions. Then, as if a switch had been cut off in her computer brain, the android woman collapsed to the deck with a heavy thud.

"Now stay dead this time. Please."

On the control bank, Polly watched a small dial rotate into place as the rocket reached the fringe of the Earth's atmosphere. Already, the air was thin and cold in the open control module.

"Five seconds to primary ignition," droned the loudspeaker voice.

"Joe!" Polly called.

The rocket hurtled toward starry space as a streak of light, then began to separate. With no time to think, Sky Captain reached into the control panel and grabbed the primary wire. With his bare hand, he snapped it free, disconnecting the circuit just as the deadly atomic engines of the third stage were about to deploy. With an explosion of sparks and an overload surge, the control panel burst into flames.

Their job done, Sky Captain and Polly took a second to hold each other close. They watched helplessly, knowing the rocket was about to explode. They might have been doomed, but the Earth would be saved.

Screeching Klaxons sounded as emergency systems engaged. "Warning: System failure! Warning: system failure!"

A high-pitched whirring sound signaled the activation of hydraulic valves. All around the diameter of the control module, new portals sprang open as Totenkopf's emergency systems activated.

"What is it?" Polly asked, dreading any last-minute surprise the mad genius might have left for them.

A series of small portals spun open in the wall next to them. Sky Captain looked at the nearest hatch, then grabbed Polly. "I don't think Totenkopf wanted to take any chances." They both dove forward.

The small dial on the control panel ratcheted into place, initiating primary ignition. Then the ascending rocket ship exploded in a terrific fireball.

36

A Fireball in the Sky
A Rescue in the Clouds
The Last Photograph

The hovercraft transport shot away from the island and over the ocean. Dex looked up at the fading fiery contrail of the rocket as it rose toward space, and then the ship bloomed into a dazzling cloud of smoke and expanding debris.

The two old Unit Eleven scientists cheered. "Sky Captain has done it! The Earth is saved."

Dex gaped in surprise and dismay, unable to say anything for several seconds. Long after the flash, the rumble of the incredible blast reached them. He swallowed hard. "He was a hero to the end. . . ." Nothing could have survived such an incredible blast.

Letting the hovercraft coast above the choppy waves, he removed a pair of binoculars he had found in a storage compartment. Apparently, Dr. Lang and Dr. Schmidt had liked to cruise over the island jungles to do prehistoric bird-watching.

Dex hefted the binoculars, focusing the lenses as he searched the sky in vain. The black clouds of ignited rocket fuel spread out as shrapnel from the vessel tumbled like meteors toward the ocean. As he swung his view slowly from side to side, an ice ball formed in his stomach.

But then he saw a tiny dot, a small object drifting down from the center of the explosion. Dex caught his breath, twisted the focusing rings, and finally spotted a small armored life pod. The pod drifted gently to Earth, held up by the scorched and ragged silk of a wide parachute.

Aboard the battered flying fortress, a young Royal Navy ensign stood on the flight deck, scanning the clouds through his own pair of binoculars. He grinned and jabbed his thumb upward. "I see them, Commander! They're alive!"

Franky Cook waited next to him, her posture perfect. She wore a clean uniform now and had straightened her cap and her eye patch. She nodded, but restrained herself from showing anything but a cool hint of relief.

She moved to the controls of a radio set and sounded a general announcement that reverberated throughout the drifting air base. "Ready assault and rescue teams. All hands on deck."

By now, most of the fires had been extinguished on board the aerial fortress. Casualties had been tallied, and the wounded taken to the sick bay. A great deal of damage had been done to the runways, and many of the Royal Navy's attack planes had been destroyed. But Franky no longer had any doubt that they could complete the obliteration of Dr. Totenkopf's remaining robots. The machine menace would be eradicated.

"Increase altitude," she called out. "Let's get out of these clouds so we can all see what we're doing."

The deck of the flying fortress teemed with activity. Her crew scrambled to mount a retrieval mission for the descending life pod. Heavily armed attack planes launched from the runways and streaked toward the mysterious island to continue mop-up operations. The giant conning tower of the flying fortress broke through the clouds, displaying the two-story-tall numeral *1* emblazoned on its front.

Franky stood on the deck, watching her loyal fighters complete their tasks smoothly and efficiently. From a cottony mass of cumulus to the east, another conning tower appeared, this one sporting the high numeral *3* on its side.

"All reinforcements have arrived as expected, Commander," the ensign said.

She smiled as a third conning tower came into view, joining the other two flying fortresses. Number seven.

The three massive hovering cities clustered together, an airborne military that could stand against the worst enemies of humanity. Wave after wave of aircraft launched from the decks, streaking away to complete their mission.

The rendezvous with Franky Cook and her flying fortress could wait. Dex changed course and maneuvered the hovering freight transport around the island toward the descending life pod. The two old scientists stood at the side of the hovercraft, watching the bright parachutes. The life pod splashed down safely in the water.

Overhead, swarms of fighter planes from the Flying Legion blackened the sky as they converged on Totenkopf's island. Thousands of aircraft filled the air with the ominous buzzing hum of a wasp's nest. The first wave broke off, and bomber squadrons descended to obliterate the target.

As Dex approached the bobbing life pod, he was startled to see giant prehistoric creatures swimming by. A spiny dorsal fin broke the water, leaving a great wake. More and more of the beasts evacuated, finding safety in the depths of the ocean.

A firestorm erupted in the center of the island as the first sequence of carpet bombing began. Military aircraft accelerated upward as a second squadron came behind them, dropping enough explosives to sterilize the landscape.

"We know Totenkopf's machines have independent programming," Dex said. "They can repair and re-build themselves. We can't leave even two pieces of metal bolted together." Later, when survey crews combed the island, they weren't likely to find anything more than hardened puddles of slag.

The hovercraft reached the bobbing life pod. The fabric of the parachute bunched around the metal vessel, drifting like seaweed. The hatch was already open to give them fresh air, but as Dex approached he saw that Sky Captain and Polly remained inside the vessel, locked in an exhausted embrace.

Hearing the hovercraft outside, the two quickly pulled apart, but Polly was still grinning. She reached into the cramped confines of the life pod and retrieved her camera. "One shot left, Joe."

"Better not waste it. What are you waiting for?" He looked out at the attacking planes of the Flying Legion and the exodus of creatures that had never before been seen by man.

Polly raised her camera and framed the smoldering island. Nearby, prehistoric monsters swam from shore. A brontosaurus raised its long neck and looked right at her. The whole spectacle seemed to be closing in on her from all points of the compass. It was an epic vision.

"Looks like you got your story," said Sky Captain.

"Editor Paley will put this on the front page. You can bet your hat on it." Polly hesitated with the cam-era, then suddenly turned to point the lens at Sky Captain. He smiled at her, blood streaking his cheek, a bruise on his forehead. "This is a better picture."

His face filled with alarm. "Polly, you . . . you . . ."

She snapped the shot on his surprised expression.

Then, satisfied, she lowered the camera. "Don't say it, Joe. You don't need to." Polly felt warm and contented.

But instead he motioned to the camera. "Lens cap."